Do you a
call dream
that date?

FROM
THE LIBRARY OF:

Do You Call That a Dream Date?

Also by Mary Anderson

CATCH ME, I'M FALLING IN LOVE

ESPECIALLY FOR GIRLS™ presents

Do You Call That a Dream Date?

MARY ANDERSON

DELACORTE PRESS/NEW YORK

To Kathleen Greer
and
Anne Adams

This book is a presentation of Especially for Girls™
Weekly Reader Books.
Weekly Reader Books offers book clubs for children from
preschool through high school.
For further information write to: **Weekly Reader Books,**
4343 Equity Drive, Columbus, Ohio 43228

Especially for Girls™ is a trademark of Weekly Reader Books.

Edited for Weekly Reader Books and published by arrangement
with Delacorte Press.

Published by
Delacorte Press
1 Dag Hammarskjold Plaza
New York, N.Y. 10017

Manufactured in the United States of America

Library of Congress Cataloging in Publication Data

Anderson, Mary [date of birth]. Do you call that a dream date?

Summary: Fourteen-year-old Jennifer overlooks the
consequences and uses an essay written by her older sister as
her entry in a school contest that is offering a date with a
famous rock star to the winner.
[1. Sisters—Fiction. 2. Plagiarism—Fiction. 3. Schools—Fiction]
I. Title.
PZ7.A5444Do 1987   [Fic]   86–908
ISBN 0-385-29488-3

Chapter One

I was in the school lunchroom, eating my egg salad on pita bread, when Liza said something extremely depressing. Liza Shapiro is my very best friend, so I can always count on her to say something that'll ruin my day.

Okay, my day was already ruined. I couldn't concentrate in any classes that morning. I was trying to figure out how to pay my sister, Carolyn, the forty-seven dollars I owed her—which she wanted immediately.

Right—*forty-seven dollars*—all because I borrowed her stinking lipstick. The sum total of my assets barely exceeded forty-seven cents!

To top it off, Liza dropped that crummy comment.

"Jenny," she whispered across the table, "I've been giving this lots of thought." Nervously, she pulled on one of her tight naturally curly curls, then watched it bounce back like a Slinky (a habit Liza's had since she was six, so

1

I've been putting up with it for eight years already). "I'm afraid our lunch table's made up of borderline cases."

"What's that mean?" I asked (knowing I shouldn't have).

"Well, I wouldn't say we were exactly misfits, because misfits can't even get a lunch table together, but we're pretty close to it. If we only had one of the in crowd sitting with us, it'd make a big difference."

"Look, Liza, twelve thirty is too early to be told I'm a misfit. Besides, my sister tells me that every day of my life, so I don't need to hear it from you."

Liza glanced over at Jeffrey, Larry, Peter, and Cassie (the other components in our misfit equation) to make certain they weren't listening. Luckily, they were in a heated conversation about the hot new rock group, Country of the Blind.

"I didn't say *misfit*," Liza corrected. "I said *borderline*. Just one really popular kid would jazz things up a lot."

At Emerson High, getting a decent lunch table together is more important than actually eating. Frankly, I thought we were doing okay. There were six of us: three boys, three girls. Okay, so two of the boys were also freshmen, but they're only slightly nerdy and they don't wear glasses. One of them, Jeffrey, is even sort of cute. And Cassie Ferguson is really smart.

I explained all this to Liza, but she wasn't impressed.

"Face it, Jenny." She shrugged. "Not one of us has pizazz." She glanced over at Beryl Fleming's table. Everyone in school called it "Beryl's Table" because they knew she could hand-pick whoever she wanted to sit with her. "If we could only get some of that group to sit with us"—she sighed wistfully—"I'm sure it'd change our entire image."

2

"Forget it. Beryl is out of our league."

Which was true. Last term, when school officials discovered asbestos in the halls, cameramen and reporters swarmed all over our school, interviewing us for the local news. Lots of us wound up on *Live at Five*, looking like jerks. Except Beryl. She hogged the camera, batted her eyes, and made barf-bag comments about teen-agers being "vulnerable." So what happened? The head of some modeling agency was watching the show and signed her to a contract. Now every day after school, she gets paid millions an hour to wear gorgeous clothes. The rest of us will probably wind up with collapsed lungs someday while Beryl smiles from the cover of *Vogue*. That girl leads a charmed life. And that thought made me feel positively terminal.

"Let's change the subject," I said, blowing my nose.

"Don't go and get psychosomatic on me, Jen. I'm merely stating a fact."

I glanced over at Beryl, too. She was reapplying her makeup with a long sable brush while four guys stared and drooled. Beryl Fleming has more cosmetics than a movie star, and I bet she got them all for *nothing*, compliments of the modeling agency. Which brings me back to the more immediate problem of that forty-seven dollars.

"Liza, have you got some money I could borrow?"

"Five dollars."

"That's not enough. I owe Carolyn forty-seven dollars."

"How come?"

"I took her lipstick."

"Wow, what was it made of, gold? How can you owe her that much for one lipstick?"

3

I'd barely figured that out myself. After all, I'd only borrowed the rotten thing. If only I'd known beforehand that Carolyn was going to institute her charming new retribution policy—payment in full for whatever I take, no matter how old or used up—payment in full for the price of the object when new.

Of course, the lipstick didn't cost that much—it was only two dollars. But after I'd used it, I threw it onto Carolyn's dresser. I guess I forgot to put the top back on, and I guess I forgot to notice that her new white wool dress was lying there. Anyway, the dress got all smeared with Coral Sunset (a color that looks lousy on me, incidentally), and the dry cleaner couldn't get it out.

"So now I owe her for the lipstick, plus forty-five dollars for the dress," I explained.

"That stinks," said Liza, "especially since you can get real great lipsticks from Consolidated Cosmetics, that mail-order place. I buy lots of stuff from them, real cheap."

"I can't. Carolyn orders from them. They've got a charming policy, too. Only one customer per family. And Carolyn's name is in their computer for life, so I can *never* order anything."

"That stinks, too."

This I already knew.

"I guess having an older sister just totally stinks, huh?"

My sentiments exactly. And Liza didn't know the half of it.

I took a bite of my pita. "These eggs must've gone bad. Maybe they came from a diseased chicken or something. They're finding poisons in everything these days, you know. It's not safe to eat or drink or *breathe* anymore."

Liza looked at me suspiciously. "Don't do your Felix

4

Ungar number on me, Jen, okay? Every time I bring up something you don't want to hear, your sinuses clog up."

"I can't help it." I sniffed. "I'm susceptible. And penniless, too. If I don't come up with that cash, Carolyn will kill me."

"How about baby-sitting? Lately, I've started charging double for two kids. Lots of people don't mind paying."

"I can't. Now that Carolyn's back home, she's taken away all my business. No one wants a fourteen-year-old when they can get a college student for the same price."

"Face it, Jen. Your sister is a waste of time."

"Tell me about it!"

"She's draining your energy from more important matters."

"Namely?"

"Namely, how we get in with the in crowd. It'd only take one of us, you know. The other will naturally follow."

"I've got more important problems. Come three o'clock, I have to face the Beaumont wrath when I tell Carolyn I'm busted."

Liza's dark eyes sparkled, which made her look like a vengeful gypsy. "Why don't you tell her to get lost?"

I had to laugh. "How do you think I start out every day? I wake up, say 'Good morning, world,' then 'Carolyn, get lost.' You're an only child, so you know absolutely nothing about human relationships. But if you're so hot for us to be more popular, *you* figure out how to do it."

"I've already made a start. I've got a date with Eddie Coleman."

Eddie was in our math class. Aside from the fact that he had one brown eye and one blue one, I hadn't noticed anything special about him. In fact, he was decidedly dull.

"If you think Eddie's going to perk up this table, you're nuts."

Liza smiled smugly. "Eddie's merely the first step on my circuitous route."

"Oh?"

"He just happens to be the best math student, so naturally he's doing all of Beryl's homework. So naturally he sometimes—"

"Sits at her table, right?"

"You got it."

"So what? Plunking next to that girl's Calvins is no great goal."

"Oh, no? She sits next to all the best-looking guys in school."

That's typical of Liza. I waste half my lunch hour thinking we're talking about one thing when we're actually talking about something totally different.

"I thought you wanted to be in solid with Beryl and the Cosmetic Creeps. But you're really talking about getting in with the best-looking guys in school. Why didn't you say so?"

"This is something a person has to say?" Liza asked.

"Well, forget it. Those guys are seniors. They wouldn't look twice at us. If they did, they'd be disappointed."

"That's right, Jen, adopt a positive attitude. It'll get you far. Know what I think? You should go home, examine yourself in the mirror, then catalog your assets. That's what I did yesterday, and know what I decided? I deserve more from life. And so do you. Face it, neither of us has had a date in *weeks*."

It's hard to believe that I felt more depressed after lunch

6

than before, but Liza had managed that nicely.

I was now an in-debt, dateless misfit with a serious sinus attack coming on.

"That's not true," I argued. "Albert Pierce called last night. He might've asked me out, if I'd given him half a chance."

Liza stared at me. "Are you crazy? The last thing you need is to be seen hanging around with Buggy Bertie."

Liza had given Albert that name in first grade, when he'd brought two roaches to school in a glass jar. He'd actually *named* them and kept them in his desk drawer. He even fed them scraps from his lunch. Of course, we thought it loathsome at the time—and it was even more disgusting when his interests progressed to mice, rats, guinea pigs, and then lizards and snakes. On Show and Tell days, Albert could always be counted on to bring in some slimy creepy-crawly that no other kid dared go near.

But Albert had been only seven then. Who knows what beasts he lived with now? Liza certainly didn't want to find out.

"I don't know why he switched to Emerson," she grumbled. "Wasn't he going to some fancy private school downtown? I think it's weird to sit in class with some guy we used to seesaw with. We can't maintain an image that way!"

"Maybe he's not so bad. I mean, we haven't actually spent time with him since sixth grade."

"When he took you on a date, right? To the Museum of Natural History, to look at bones. Face it, Jen; guys like that don't get better. He's a creep. It's bad enough he's in three of our classes. Don't ruin your social life by going out with him."

7

"Oh, he didn't actually ask me. I just thought he might've, if I'd given him half a chance."

"Well, take my advice and don't. And speaking of the devil," she added, "I think I see Buggy Bertie heading our way."

Liza was right. I hate saying lousy things about people who suddenly pop up. Of course, it wasn't actually me saying the lousy things, but I felt embarrassed just the same.

I mean, maybe Albert wasn't all that bad. Of course, he could've done with a decent haircut and a new pair of sneakers, and he desperately needed some clothes that fit him properly. But I'd always thought he had a certain charm—different, but appealing.

The rest of the kids at our table were winding up their heated discussion of heavy metal versus new wave and were throwing away their sandwich wrappers when Albert ambled over.

Liza smiled at him as if he were her long-lost friend. "How're you doing, Albert?"

"Okay."

"Too bad we didn't notice you earlier. Lunch period's over now, isn't it?"

"I guess."

"Well, another day," she said brightly. "We can talk over old times."

He smiled. "Sure, that'd be great. I don't know many kids here yet, and—"

"Oh, but you will, I'm sure. Emerson High is just one big happy family."

"Really?"

I must've been standing with my mouth hanging open, because Liza poked me in the ribs. "Well," she said, "we'd

8

better go now. If you're late for Mr. Campbell's biology class, he'll dissect your vital organs."

"That's why I stopped by," said Albert, staring straight at me. "I coudn't help noticing that you're having trouble in that class, Jenny."

"That's right." I sniffed. "I've missed the last few assignments. My sinuses. I mean, I was out sick."

"I know."

Albert's yellow-green eyes seemed to twinkle in my direction. They were really very nice eyes, but after Liza's conversation they suddenly reminded me of frog embryos. "I'm not too great in biology anyway," I added.

"I noticed. Well, if you need any help catching up, let me know. We could get together sometime after school, or anytime."

"Isn't that sweet," said Liza, pushing me toward the lunchroom door. "That's really sweet, isn't it, Jenny? I hope that offer stands for me, too, Albert. When it comes to cutting up cadaverous amphibians, I really miss the mark."

As Albert ran his fingers through his hair, he looked confused. "Yeah—sure, Liza, anytime."

"Thanks a million."

"What was that all about?" I asked as she hurried me up the stairs. "If you think Albert's such a creep, why pour on the charm?"

"He may be a creep, but he's a smart one. And you're not the only rotten biology student. By midterm, Albert's help may come in handy."

Liza's my best friend, but at times she can be awfully manipulative!"

Chapter Two

I decided to take Liza's advice. As soon as I got home from school, I'd survey my assets.

Fortunately, I had the apartment to myself. Both Mom and Carolyn were still in class. It was always fun to be alone in the apartment.

See, I was never raised as one of these latchkey kids. Up until last year, when Mom and Dad got divorced, my mother was *always* home—cooking, cleaning, sewing— you name it. In fact, I thought our family was some sort of throwback to the Waltons. There was never any real privacy.

Which is strange, because growing up in an apartment in Manhattan can actually be more private than living out on the prairie. No one bothers anyone else, unless they want to be bothered. There are people in our building I've known since childhood, yet I don't actually know them at all—just to nod hello to in the elevator—which is fine with me.

One of my biggest treats is to come home to an empty apartment and spread out. Oh, that doesn't mean I don't miss Dad; I do. But he was never home during the day anyhow.

My dad lives in Seattle now. It was one of those friendly divorces that everyone says don't exist, but I really think they do. Dad works for an oil company and always traveled a lot anyway, so things don't seem that much different. He calls several times a week to ask about my allergies and junk like that.

Carolyn says I'm merely blocking out the trauma and feelings of rejection that I've subconsciously sublimated, and that I'll spend years in analysis later on if I don't admit my abject misery now. But I think that's part of the dopey psychological jargon she's suddenly adopted.

How I wish my sister had stayed away at college! For a few brief months, I lived in bliss. Suddenly, my life started shaping up, you know? Even my sinuses began to drain!

And best of all, I had a room to myself. Since *birth*, I'd had to share a room with Carolyn and live on halfsies—half a room, half a dresser, half a closet, half a TV—on which I never got to see *my* favorite shows.

Half a life, actually.

Not to mention always being called "Carolyn's kid sister" (as if it were my first name or something) and getting booted out of my half-room whenever her putrid friends came over. But I guess all kid sisters have to live with stuff like that.

But no one else has had to live with *Carolyn*.

Even I didn't have to for a few glorious months.

11

I was in heaven when she packed her bags and took the plane to Oberlin College in Ohio. I'd had a moment of panic when she was considering Sarah Lawrence, which is close enough to come home on weekends; but luckily, she opted for a school farther away.

I envisioned four glorious years in which I'd be allowed to mature at my own pace. By the time she graduated, I'd be away in college, so I'd never have to see her crummy face again.

But the best laid plans—you know.

Well, it was great while it lasted.

I tacked *my* favorite posters on the wall—Duran Duran and Country of the Blind. I listened to *my* favorite music, and I let junk pile up under my bed.

In fact, my bed was one of the very best features of having Carolyn go away. We had two single platform beds, which I moved together to make a big king-size one, just like I'd seen in magazines. Only mine didn't look like the ones in the magazines, with puffy down comforters. The top of mine was stacked with books, makeup, candy wrappers, and clothes I'd never bothered to hang up, but there was still lots of room to stretch out at night.

With Mom back in school, she'd stopped bothering to clean like a madman. So for the first time in my life I had *my* room, which I kept as messy as I liked.

Listen, I'm not embarrassed to say I'm a slob. Hey, we live in a free country, right? Those compelled to be neat can go ahead. On the other hand, those of us who love to live in friendly, messy clutter should be left alone. Personally, I feel there's something very cozy about huge familiar lumps scattered all over my bed. If I wake up in the middle of the night, I can always grab a cookie or read a magazine without even getting up.

I mean, I *could* before. Now when I wake up at night, I have to struggle through the dark to find the lamp switch. When I turn it on, all I see is Carolyn sleeping in the opposite corner. And I *know* she's lying there dreaming up new ways to make my life a nightmare.

Carolyn says I've taken sibling rivalry to ridiculous extremes, but I really hate her guts. I guess everyone at Oberlin must've, too, because she didn't last more than one term. According to her, dorm life was "shallow" and the constant parties a "bore" and if she ever sees another HAVE A NICE DAY poster, she'll puke. So now she's a premed student at Columbia and more obnoxious than ever, since she's decided to specialize in psychiatry.

I wasn't home more than five minutes when Liza called.

"Have you started yet?" she asked.

"I just walked in the door."

"Well, I forgot to tell you the most important part. Get a pad and pencil and make two columns. On one side, write, I DO HAVE, and on the other, I DON'T HAVE. Okay?"

"Did you make up this quiz or what?"

"Of course not. It's very scientific. I read it in *Glamour* magazine. Call me back when you're finished."

I got out a pad and pencil, then stood in front of the closet mirror.

I stared at myself, then stared at the pad.

Under I DON'T HAVE, I wrote: two heads.

Under I DO HAVE, I wrote: two pimples.

So far, so good.

After a while, I really got into the swing of it. An hour later, my survey was complete.

13

For the record, I don't have:

>   any major fat parts (except maybe for my
>   upper thighs)
>   braces, tics, or twitches
>   chapped lips
>   big feet, hangnails, or split ends
>   hammer toes
>   bad posture or an outie belly button

and I do have:

>   large blue eyes, not too close together
>   a halfway decent smile
>   a small waist
>   legs that look good in shorts
>   naturally blond hair
>   ears that don't stick out
>   well-shaped, unplucked eyebrows

This test wasn't half bad. I didn't exactly feel like a world-beater, but there was no reason I couldn't compete with Beryl Fleming. I was just as pretty, just as tall, just as—

My newly found bubble of self-confidence suddenly burst when I noticed Carolyn's reflection behind me. I guess I'd gotten so caught up in my self-image, I hadn't heard her come in.

Putting her books on the desk, she noticed my pad and picked it up. "What's this?" she asked scornfully. "It looks suspiciously like those semipsych, pop-culture quizzes in the fashion rags."

"None of your business," I said, grabbing the pad. "But

if you must know, I'm surveying my assets."

"That shouldn't take you long. You forgot to write the most important thing in that 'Do Have' column—and it better be forty-seven dollars."

"Look, Carolyn, I don't have the cash. It won't kill you to wait."

"But it will kill you. Give me that money by the end of the week, or you can add something else to that dopey quiz—because you *Don't Have* much longer to live. Now straighten up in here, so I can do my homework."

Charming, right? I wish I could say Carolyn's appearance is as miserable as her personality, but she's actually very pretty. In fact, she reminds me of those Miss America contestants. You know the ones, with all the hair and big white teeth, who are always studying to be brain surgeons. They're in their teens, but they all look *thirty*. Like someone's mother, you know? I guess that's what I mean. Chronologically, Carolyn may still be a teen-ager, but at heart she's middle-aged.

"Did you start dinner yet?" she asked.

"I haven't had time."

"Jennifer, you know Mom has late classes on Tuesday. Whoever gets home first is supposed to start dinner. What's on the menu? Did you go to the grocery store, like my note said?"

"What note?"

"The one tacked on the fridge, you imbecile."

"Well, I didn't go into the kitchen. I was too busy."

"I know, surveying your assets. Well, that should only have taken half a second. Although your physical attributes are minor, they're gargantuan compared to your mental capabilities, which are decidedly Neanderthal."

Unfortunately, the only reply I could think of was "Same to you, jerk."

"Now that you've expressed yourself in that superior manner, kindly get into the kitchen and see if there's something edible for dinner. I've got a term paper due in the morning, and I can't think on an empty stomach."

Between Mom and Carolyn, the house was crawling with term papers.

"Well, what'll I make?"

"I don't care," she sighed, "as long as it's not tuna casserole!"

Chapter Three

I made tuna casserole.

Well, it's the only thing I knew how to cook, because it comes from cans. It gave me a lift, fulfilling my kitchen duties while making Carolyn barfo. Two birds, you know.

Mom looked frazzled when she got home, like those harried housewives in cartoons, with little wisps of hair sticking out all over. She'd never looked that exhausted when she *was* a full-time housewife. But Mom is determined to get her master's in social work by the end of next term even if it kills her.

Or me.

I sincerely hope I don't get crazed if I'm divorced at forty. Since the breakup, Mom has changed a lot. She's talking about hiking alone through Scotland next summer. Used to be, when we'd spend the summers upstate, she'd never even leave the house. She's also joined a health club and a computer dating service. I think she plans to turn into a totally different person. But first she wants to get her MSW and a lifetime civil service job.

But I'm adjusting okay. Who cares if the house is disorganized? Well, maybe I do overreact when Mom complains about her homework. I mean, she never sympathized with me when I didn't get assignments done, so why should I pity her?

At least one thing hasn't changed. Dinner has always been the time to hash over the day's events and problems. In fact, we used to call it "hashtime."

Carolyn couldn't wait to bring up the subject of money again.

"Hasn't that been resolved yet?" asked Mom. "You two were screaming about it all day yesterday."

"I never scream," said Carolyn. "And it hasn't been resolved because your daughter is a pauper."

That was Carolyn's latest obnoxious habit: referring to me as "your daughter" or "your youngest child" whenever she spoke to Mom—as if I were too loathsome to address directly.

"Well, I'm putting an end to it right now," said Mom. "Jenny, I'll advance you the money to pay Carolyn. But I expect you to repay me in six weeks. I can't study in this house with you two at each other's throats."

Carolyn was furious. "Mother, you've negated my entire object lesson. Jennifer has to become responsible for her actions. She has no discipline. That's why she never completes a task."

"That's not true. I made dinner."

"That's right," Mom agreed. "Exactly what is it we're eating?"

"Tuna casserole. Well, almost. There were no peas, so I

substituted canned corn. And we had no potato chips, so I put in pretzels instead."

Mom mushed it around on her plate. "Yes, well, it's very—interesting."

"It's vile," said Carolyn, "and the way that child gets away with things is even more so. I was planning to wear that white dress tomorrow night before she ruined it. John's taking me to a concert, and that dress would've been perfect."

I found it hard to believe that Carolyn had a steady boyfriend. A nice one, too. In fact, I'd had a minor crush on John Linhart for a while, until I realized that anyone involved with Carolyn must have some fatal flaw. I just hadn't found it yet.

Mom tried being diplomatic. "But white's not flattering on you, anyway; it drains your color. Wear your red dress instead, dear. Now, to change the subject, how're you both doing with school?"

"I'm doing okay," I lied, ignoring the fifty-two I'd just received in math, not to mention the thirty-seven in biology.

"Professor Maxwell says my work has been outstanding," Carolyn bragged. "He hasn't read my latest psych paper yet, but he loved the title: 'The Ramifications of the Beatles on a Generation.'"

"Sounds stupid to me," I said. "How could a rock group affect a whole generation?"

"Profoundly, that's how. The Beatles were never a mere rock group. They were both the touchstone and turning point of the entire culture of the sixties, and my paper elaborates on that idea. Oh, and I've also volunteered to help Professor Maxwell with a study he's doing in adolescent psychology. He has some fascinating theories. He's pulling strings to get me a special baby-sitting job after school."

"What's so hot about baby-sitting?" I asked.

"This wouldn't be sitting for an ordinary child. Professor Maxwell only works with parents who've enrolled their children in the Better Baby Institute, parents who feel the capabilities of preschoolers have yet to be discovered. Toddlers enrolled in the program can do fantastic things, like adding, subtracting, and recognizing major works of art. Which makes them all superior to you, birdbrain."

"Yeah, well, I bet they can't change their own diapers, or they wouldn't need you."

"Sounds fascinating," said Mom. "Maybe if kids had more intellectual stimulation during infancy, they wouldn't grow up antisocial and rebellious."

"That's the professor's point exactly," said Carolyn. "A properly intellectually nurtured child is the hallmark of superior parenting."

"That may be true," said Mom, "but if it were a reality, no one would need social workers. Listen, don't put me out of business before I start."

"Mother," said Carolyn dramatically, "you'll be happy to know my future is finally resolved. I'm going to specialize in infant psychiatry. It's a burgeoning field."

Mom blinked and said she knew very few babies who needed shrinks, but Carolyn was insistent. Apparently a few months of studying with flakey Professor Maxwell had changed her mind about eveything.

"Lots of studies have been done already," she continued. "Babies deprived of physical contact actually suffer depression. They become moody, temperamental, and unresponsive. As a matter of fact, I think that's the root of Jennifer's problem."

"What does that mean?" asked Mom.

"Well, she was a premature baby. Those three weeks in an incubator, denied normal human contact, could've caused irreparable harm. It might be the reason she's such an incredible slob."

"That's nonsense, Carolyn. Your sister received the same amount of nurturing as you did. Picking up her filthy socks is her own responsibility!"

"She gets away with murder. Her entire generation does."

"*Her* generation? I thought you two shared that, at least."

"Hardly. Adolescents of today are nothing like we were."

Like I said, my sappy sister is actually middle-aged.

While she and Mom continued arguing, I suddenly saw the bright side of the conversation. If Carolyn got a job baby-sitting superbrains, that'd leave the field clear for me to get jobs in the building again, stitting with mere mortals. Which meant I could actually pay Mom back in six weeks.

"I think Carolyn's career ideas are wonderful," I said, smiling sweetly. "And I wish her luck."

Mom was almost speechless. "Well, I guess that settles that—for now. Let's finish this whatever-it-is so we can all do our homework."

I was halfway through putting down all the wrong answers in geometry when Liza called.

"Well, how'd you score? Pardon the expression."

"Not bad. I guess you're right. There's no reason we can't make it into the big leagues, if Beryl doesn't throw us any curve balls. What should we do to attract those gorgeous guys? Fall at their feet?"

"Only as a last resort. First, I suggest a major beauty tone-up. Come to my house after school tomorrow and bring every cosmetic you own."

Chapter Four

The next day, Liza and I exchanged lists.

"Hey, you wrote down flabby thighs, too," I said. "Maybe we should work on those first?"

"No, in my case I think it's ethnic or generic or something."

"You mean genetic."

"Right. Anyway, let's skip it. I think our faces deserve the immediate attention. Let's see what you've got." Liza surveyed my array of cosmetics. "*Four* Calvin Klein lipsticks? They're expensive."

"No, they're Carolyn's. I put them on the radiator so they'd get mushy and she wouldn't want them anymore. Then I stuck them in the fridge to reshape them. See this blush brush? I soaked it in the sink so it'd get ratty. When she threw it out, I used the blow-dryer on it."

"How marvelously sneaky," said Liza with admiration.

"I try."

"Is any of this stuff actually yours?"

"Sure. I bought the eyeshadow and the liner. But the Revlon foundation was Carolyn's, too. I suggested she buy a darker shade, because I knew she'd never wear it. Hey, you want to put purple eyeshadow on our eyelids?"

"Sure, let's shoot the works. And I'll try a depilatory on my arms and upper lip. Have you noticed I'm starting to look like Groucho Marx?"

"Hairiness isn't one of my problems. Because I'm blond, you don't see it."

While we watched the end of *General Hospital*, I covered my eyelids with my new eyeshadow, Misty Mauve, and Liza smeared hair-remover on her arms and upper lips. After ten minutes, I got worried. "Liza, you'd better wash that stuff off. Once Stacey Kirkpatrick left it on too long and she became a giant scab!"

She went running for the bathroom. "Now you tell me!" Luckily, she made it in time, before her skin started peeling.

After that, we experimented with hairdos. Liza pulled mine back into one long French braid. "Just like Beryl was wearing yesterday," she explained.

I tried doing something with hers, too, but every time I piled her curls on top of her head, a million little ones came trickling down. "But it looks nice that way," I said, "like a Greek goddess."

Then we stared at ourselves in the mirror.

"What do you think, Jen? Are we new women, or the same old ones in a different package?"

I suddenly realized what was missing. "A color rinse. Your hair'd look great with henna highlights, and I could

24

put some streaks in mine."

Liza loved the idea, so we ran out to Pathmark on Broadway and bought L'Oreal color rinses. That purchase nearly wiped me out financially, but what the heck, I'm worth it.

Fortunately, I'd told Mom I wouldn't be home for dinner, so we had all the time in the world to become gorgeous. Back at Liza's house, we tinted each other's hair. Pouring on all that glop messed up our makeup, so we had to redo it all. This time, I really laid on that Misty Mauve.

We were both so pleased with the results, we decided to celebrate with burgers at Charlie's. That's a place on Columbus Avenue, popular with high-school kids. Aside from their giant hamburgers, they've got a fabulous ice cream counter. They throw scoops of ice cream down on a marble slab, then mix in whatever fixings you like: chocolate chip cookies, Junior Mints, M&M's—the works. One scoop may add up to a zillion calories, but it sure is delicious.

Lots of kids from Emerson High hang out there. But without a doubt the best feature of Charlie's is that boys from PCS—Professional Children's School—hang out there, too. PCS is just blocks away from Emerson. It's a big-deal private school for kids in show business who model, act, or dance. What a deal they've got going! They can take off for months when they're making movies on location and have their schoolwork mailed to them. Not bad! Most of the guys are probably dead from the neck up, but they're all hunks, so who cares?

Naturally, since Beryl had become a miniceleb, she hangs out with them. This day was no exception. When we arrived, Beryl was draped across the piano looking gorgeous while some equally gorgeous guy banged out an R&B tune. That's another special feature at Charlie's. There's a beat-up old piano in the corner with a sign above it: FEEL FREE TO TICKLE THE IVORIES. It's one of the few places in the neighborhood where teen-agers don't get hustled out the door when they walk in. You can hang around at the counter for hours and just order a soda. Charlie, the owner, is more interested in having a fun time himself than in making a fortune (even though he is).

We picked a corner table near the piano. Liza thought the pink spotlight over there would "enhance" the new auburn highlights in her hair.

"Cast an eye at the guy playing," she panted.

"I noticed. I think his muscles have muscles. I'll bet he works out every day. Haven't we seen him in a Dr. Pepper commercial?"

"I've seen him in my *dreams!*" Liza took out a mirror to check her hair. "Not bad. One of us should rate at least a look."

"Not With Ms. Fleming nearby." Now there were *three* gorgeous guys vying for Beryl's attention. "Shouldn't there be a quota system?" I grumbled. "She's got three and we've got none." Two of the guys definitely looked like seniors, but the third, equally cute, looked about sixteen. "Let's hope at least one of them notices us."

"Well, *someone* just noticed us," whispered Liza, "by the name of Albert Pierce."

Albert, looking curiously self-conscious, had just walked in.

"Let's ask him over, Jen. Who knows? Maybe a little

healthy competition will spark these guys' interest."

Liza waved in Albert's direction, and he smiled and hurried over to our table.

"Hi, guys. A nice-looking place. I heard about it at school and thought I'd check it out."

"Sit down," I said. "We're just about to order burgers. What about you?"

"None for me, unless they have a tofu burger. I've become a vegetarian."

Liza frowned. I knew all too well her opinion on *that* subject! Macho men ate meat, not celery stalks. Only wimps or fanatics ate bean sprouts and tofu.

"A vegetarian?" I asked. "When did that happen?"

"Last year. I read something Oscar Wilde wrote about people who hunt animals. He said they were 'the unspeakable after the uneatable.' It got me thinking, and I've never been able to look at meat since."

"Really?" said Liza sarcastically as the waitress came for our order. "Well, we all know Oscar Wilde was weird, don't we? I mean, that character of his, Dorian Gray, did some pretty kinky things!"

Liza was an English lit expert, so she should know. But now it made me feel like a cannibal to order a burger.

"Maybe I'll have something else," I said.

"Don't be silly," said Liza. "Two burgers, medium rare, with lots of blood-red juice! And two diet Cokes, please."

"That's right," said Albert, "don't be embarrassed. Meat's part of our culture. It's been romanticized, like smoking; especially beef. I'll have a malted and some French fries, thanks."

As the waitress left, Liza glanced longingly toward the trio at the piano while Albert continued his theory.

"I think it all started with the Western," he explained. "All those tough cowboys driving cattle across the plains. A real he-man image, right? Who stopped to think that all those cows would be chopped to bits when they reached the end of the trail? *That's* where beef got its image. But pork has never had the same popularity. Wanna know why?"

"No, but I'm dying to," said Liza.

"Because all those cattle herders would've been called 'pigboys' instead. Their image would've gone right out the window."

I found that an interesting theory: peculiar, but still interesting.

"Maybe you're right," I agreed. "I mean, there are lots of phrases that give meat a positive image—getting a 'meaty part' and 'beefing things up,' stuff like that."

"Beefcake," Liza added, still drooling at the other guys.

When my burger arrived, it seemed to have a face, so I pushed it away. Besides, my eyes were starting to tear. I couldn't tell if it was another sinus attack or an allergy to the purple eyeshadow.

"Want a tissue?" Albert offered, digging into his pocket. As he did, some seeds and dried things spilled out.

"A little snack?" asked Liza snidely. "What *is* that garbage?"

Albert turned red. "Birdseed. There's a sparrow with a broken wing outside the window in math class. Haven't you seen it?"

Liza'd had enough. "Albert, would you mind getting the waitress and asking for another Coke?"

"Sure."

Once he'd gone, she suggested we ditch him.

"We can't do that. Besides, you're the one who invited him over."

"I know, but all this henna and depilatory is being wasted on that weirdo. You'll excuse the expression, but I'm taking the bull by the horns and crashing in on Beryl's fun."

By now, Beryl and her triple catch were leafing through the pages of *Variety*. All PCS kids read that paper as if it were sacred because they're always going up for auditions and stuff. It has all the latest showbiz news.

Liza eased over to the piano and quickly wedged herself into the conversation. Some guy from Emerson standing by the counter nudged Albert and they started talking, so I sat alone at the table, nibbling on his French fries.

Then I noticed Carolyn walk in.

No one over eighteen ever set foot in Charlie's. What was she doing, checking up on me?

I ran toward the door before anyone noticed her.

"What are *you* doing here?" I asked.

"Mom said I'd probably find you in this place," she said, glancing around. "What would you call this decor? Early nightmare?"

Well, I was mortified. Carolyn had probably come to do another one of her sappy psychological surveys. She'd already pestered half my friends with embarrassing questions about "their adolescence." If she pulled that number in Charlie's, I'd be a laughingstock!

"Beat it," I said diplomatically.

"Relax, this is strictly a business call. It's an emergency. I had to talk to you immediately."

"What's wrong?"

"Nothing. In fact, everything's great, if you'll cooperate.

Professor Maxwell got me that baby-sitting job I mentioned."

"So what?"

"I'll be sitting for a four-year-old boy, Jason, who lives on Morningside Drive."

"Who cares?"

"Jennifer, be silent and listen. Jason's mother takes childrearing seriously and insists that I have a backup sitter available at all times. In order to get the job, I have to tell her immediately, so what do you say?"

"About what?"

"Being my backup. Naturally, you'd never actually care for the child. It's merely an emergency contingency plan."

What a hoot. Carolyn was asking me for a favor. Why should I let her off the hook? Let her squirm. Wriggle. Let her lose her crummy job, for all I cared.

"It pays five dollars an hour," she added.

"It's a deal. Now scram, okay?"

As Carolyn turned to leave, she stared back at me. "Jennifer, do they still beat out erasers in high school?"

"How do I know? Why?"

"Well, your hair looks like it's filled with chalk dust. Maybe it's the dreadful lighting in this den. Your eyes look all bloodshot, too. They don't serve alcohol in here, do they?"

"No, now *beat it!*"

I could feel my eyes begin to itch. I guess Misty Mauve isn't hypoallergenic. Pretty soon my nose would probably be as purple as my eyelids. My scalp started to feel itchy, too. Had I left that hair dye on too long?

By now, Albert was back at the table finishing his malted.

"What's wrong?" he asked. "You don't look so hot."

Terrific. My big makeover was turning into a disaster.

"I'm okay, just a minor allergy."

"You still get those? I remember once in fourth grade when you blew up like a tomato!"

I began to think Liza was right. Hanging around a guy you've shared the chicken-pox period with could really ruin your image.

"That was years ago," I insisted.

Albert drowned his French fries in ketchup. "Oh. Well, maybe you're coming down with something, then."

"Am I really?" A bad allergic reaction could make my eyes swell like balloons. Suddenly, I couldn't wait to get home and wash everything off.

"You really should eat your hamburger. After all, the cow gave his life. I know they say slaughterhouses are humane, but I think those two words are contradictory terms, don't you?"

I was getting real tired of hearing about dead animals. My stomach wasn't feeling so great either.

I gestured to Liza that I wanted to leave. She signaled for me to come over. I shook my head. She looked like she'd broken the ice with the PCS guys, but I didn't care. They were the last people I wanted to see me now.

"Don't go now, Jen," she said as I headed toward the door. "I'm finally making some points here. One of those guys actually *noticed* me. His name is Chuck, wouldn't you know! He had a bit part in a soap last week that might turn into something. I lied and said it was my favorite show, and he really came to life. If I play my cards right, he might actually ask me out."

"That's great, really, but I've got to get out of here. My

face is starting to feel crawly."

"Yeah, you look strange, sort of splotchy. But it's probably just the lighting in here. C'mon over by the piano. Beryl isn't half bad, if you can manage to ignore her."

"No, I'm leaving. Call me tonight and let me know how things turn out."

I was soaking in a baking soda bath when Liza called. (Baking soda works wonders when I'm itching.)

Mom'd bought this great cordless phone, so I was able to talk without leaving the tub. "How'd it go?" I asked.

"Great. Chuck and I really hit it off. He loves my hair. Don't tell anyone, but he uses the same henna rinse. And mousse, too, can you believe it? Those guys at PCS are really into stuff like that. But he's not strange, only conceited."

"Don't mention cosmetics," I said, scratching. "Did he ask you for a date?"

"I'm not sure. He invited me to watch him work out at the health club. Would you call that a date?"

"I don't think so."

"Chuck said he'd be at Charlie's after school tomorrow. He's bringing his eight-by-ten glossies for me to see."

"I don't call that a date either."

"Maybe not, but it's a start. I'd say our beauty makeover paid off."

"Not for me it didn't."

"Sorry. But listen, I've got news that'll give you a lift for sure. It's just about the most spectacular thing that's ever happened. Beryl was reading about it in *Variety*—which disproves your theory. Remember? You bet she didn't know how to read. That was very unkind, Jen. Beryl's grades aren't any rottener than yours."

"Oh, really? Sounds like you two have gotten quite chummy."

"Well, being beautiful doesn't necessarily make her a bad person. I'm only saying she's not as stupid as you thought."

"So that's the fantastic news that's supposed to thrill me?"

"Of course not. The fantastic news is—wait, are you sitting down?"

"Lying, actually. I'm soaking in the tub."

"Well, don't drown or anything when you hear this. There's going to be a contest. The most fabulous contest in the entire world. And the most fabulous part is that only girls from Emerson High are eligible. Bet you'll never guess what the prize is going to be."

"Okay, what?"

"The winner gets a date with—hold your breath—Matt Gates!"

"*Matt Gates!*" I shouted, nearly dropping the phone into the tub. "Are you serious?"

"Deadly. There was this big article about it in *Variety*. The news'll probably be all over school soon, but I wanted you to know right away. Isn't that spectacular?"

It was *unbelievable!* Matt Gates was the incredibly gorgeous lead singer of the rock group Country of the Blind. Their first album went to the top of the charts overnight. I'd seen their one and only video on MTV at least a million times. Powerful! In one year, the group had come from nowhere and shot to superstardom.

Every girl in school had the group's album, not to mention Matt Gates buttons and notebooks. Lots of them also wore silver cords around their necks, just like he did in his act. Matt was the hottest English import since the Beatles.

Yeah, there was an epidemic of Matt Gates mania. Well, the entire group was gorgeous: Tom, the bassist; Rick, on the keyboard; and Bryan, the drummer. But Matt, with his guitar, was definitely the superstar of the act, even though no one had actually seen his entire face. Matt never appeared in public or before a camera without large black sunglasses. Even in his life-size pinup poster—which hung above my bed—he's wearing those glasses and the silver cord around his neck that has become his trademark.

I'd tried getting a ticket to their concert at Madison Square Garden in September, but the lines went clear to Jersey and scalpers were charging a hundred bucks! Any girl at Emerson would've laid down and died for a look at Gates in the flesh. But a *date*—well, that was awesome!

"Tell me all the details. When, where, and how?"

"It's some big publicity thing, I guess," said Liza. "The group's got a new video coming out soon, I think. Chuck knows all about this showbiz stuff, and he says it's just promotion—a great way to get a fortune in free publicity. But who cares? The important thing is, one of us is actually going to date Matt Gates. And if that isn't the world's best dream date, I don't know what is."

"But how'd he choose Emerson High?"

"He didn't actually choose it. I think they threw the names of lots of schools into a hat, and we were the winner."

"Fantastic. But what kind of contest is it? Do we pick a number like the lottery?"

"Don't know. The paper didn't mention those details,

but I guess we'll all have an equal chance. Isn't it exciting?"

It was more than exciting; it was monumental.

I could hardly wait to find out more.

Chapter Five

Two days later, Emerson High went crazy.

Notification of the contest had been on the local news the night before.

Naturally, students'll use any excuse to tear themselves away from the old books, but this was a *great* one. By ten o'clock, kids were stampeding the hallways, and everyone knew what was up.

Even some of the teachers—those who'd heard of Matt Gates—were excited. Mr. Corbett, the principal, practically had his door knocked down as we all demanded further details.

"They'll be forthcoming!" he insisted.

After lunch, a sign had been posted in the hall:

ALL DETAILS OF THE UPCOMING CONTEST, TO BE ANNOUNCED AT A FULL ASSEMBLY IN THE AUDI-TORIUM AT 2 P.M.

Needless to say, no one paid attention during classes, and the teachers gave up trying to keep order.

At two o'clock, we practically burst our way through those auditorium doors.

Old Corbett had assembled the heads of all the departments onstage, and he was in the center at the podium. Our principal is about a thousand years old, so I'm sure he'd never heard of Country of the Blind, which made the whole thing kind of funny.

"Attention, please," he shouted. "This morning I received a special delivery letter from the Sandpiper Recording Company, who have under contract a group referred to as Country of the Blind. No doubt you've all heard of them."

There was a momentary uproar as everyone got hysterical.

"Yes, no doubt. This letter details the intentions of the aforementioned musical group. It is their desire to hold a unique contest. The winner of this competition will be a female high-school student. And the prize will be an all-expense-paid evening with the individual known as Matt Gates."

All the girls went wild. I think Liza and I cheered louder than anyone.

Corbett shouted for order, then continued. "Male students won't be totally ignored in this competition. As part of the prize, Country of the Blind will make a personal appearance at Emerson to greet the winner, and an autograph session will follow."

Now the guys seemed interested, too.

"Does that mean they're gonna play for us?" they shouted.

"There's no mention of a performance in this letter, but perhaps they will."

What followed that remark could be classified as utter hysteria. Kids stood on the seats and threw their books in the air. Poor old Corbett nearly had a heart attack.

"Quiet, *please*. I'm sure you're all interested in how Emerson was selected for this honor. All New York public schools in the five boroughs were in a preliminary competition. Each was given a random number, and Emerson High was the winner. This musical group, which I'm assured is very fine indeed, wishes to show its appreciation to the young people of the city, who first acknowledged their talents. And I must say, I find that most commendable."

"Can't Corbett stop blabbing and get to the point?" Liza grumbled.

I agreed. "Yeah, there's only one important fact in this deal. How's the winner to be chosen?"

Lots of kids shouted out that question, but Corbett ignored it.

"Normally, I might question the efficacy of such a contest disrupting the educational process of our school, or perhaps even creating an adverse competitive atmosphere. But I've conferred with Mr. Banks, head of the music department, and Mrs. Henley, our English department head. We all agree that the contest's stipulations tend to enhance the learning experience here at Emerson."

Learning experience? That didn't sound too good.

"Because our school may have been picked at random, but the winner of this contest will not. All female students who wish to participate must submit an essay to Mrs. Henley within the next two weeks. This essay must consist of one thousand words or more, entitled 'What

Your Music Means to Me.' At the end of two weeks, Mrs. Henley will select the finest submission, after which the winner will be personally congratulated by Matt Gates during a special presentation on May seventeenth."

Translated, that meant we'd have to *work* to win.

Now, instead of cheers, groans filled the auditorium. No one liked this idea. Lots of kids like me—lousy in English—were underwhelmed, to say the least.

"Well, maybe writing an essay won't be so terrible," said Liza.

"Easy for you to say," I grumbled. "You get nineties in English. I don't stand a chance."

It wasn't fair. I would've walked barefoot over burning coals for a date with Matt Gates. But an essay? Well, forget it. I was out of the running before I started.

Corbett prattled on. "I hope this will inspire all you young ladies to achieve a degree of excellence in your writing. Mrs. Henley has kindly volunteered to confer with any student who feels she needs assistance expressing herself grammatically and succinctly."

Sarah Henley smiled from the stage and nodded. She was the second-oldest human in the school. She loved to confiscate kids' Walkmans. I think the hottest music she knew was Lawrence Welk. Oh yeah, she'd be lots of help!

"Might I add something?" she asked. "Your principal and I agree that there will be no losers in this contest. All girls entering will have the satisfaction of knowing they have attempted the most difficult of literary forms: the essay. Thank you."

As we filed out of the auditorium, I discovered that no one was thrilled with the rules. The guys thought it made Matt Gates sound like a jerk, coming up with a crummy contest like that. And the girls, even those good in English, didn't know what to write about.

"What're we supposed to say?" complained Cassie. "When I listen to Matt Gates, I go crazy! I certainly can't write that."

Everyone agreed the contest rules were stupid. All the girls felt they didn't stand a chance.

That gave me a lift. Maybe I wasn't out of the running after all!

For the next few days, Charlie's must've turned into a ghost town. Most of the girls from Emerson went straight home after school to work on their essays. So did I.

I'd sit in my room, staring at my Matt Gates poster. I watched his video, *Snakey Highway*, every time it was scheduled, and I listened to his album *Full Disclosure* dozens of times. I immersed myself in Country of the Blind, hoping to become inspired.

I didn't.

Whenever I sat down to tackle my essay, all I could think of writing was, I've got to win this contest, I've got to win this contest. Hardly literary!

The stakes were really high. Winning the date would be fabulous enough; but it would be only the beginning of a fabulous new life. I'd become the most popular, famous girl at Emerson, and I'd have my pick of the guys. And who knows what else? I mean, Beryl's modeling career started with asbestos, so this could lead to something even bigger, right?

Pictures in the paper.

Interviews.

Maybe even an appearance on a talk show.

Yeah, winning the contest might be the beginning of fantastic fame and fortune.

So I *had* to be the one.

Who was I kidding? Winning also meant knowing how to put two words together. A senior English student was bound to pull it off.

Liza didn't agree.

"Listen, we all stand a chance. Maybe Matt Gates is looking for sincerity or a sense of humor, not a brilliant brain."

"You forget one tiny fact. Sarah Henley is actually picking the winner, not Matt Gates."

"Right. Well, maybe you *are* in trouble, but at least you should try. I'm not giving up. Chuck has promised to help me. He plays the guitar, too, and he knows lots of musical terms, so I'm filling up my essay with tons of technical stuff. Then if I win, I've promised to get Chuck an intro to the band. That's called networking."

"That's not fair!"

"Who says? In this deal, it's every woman for herself. You can figure out a way to impress Henley, too."

"How?"

"How should I know? You're my best friend, Jen, but you've gotta do this on your own. I want to win as much as you do."

So it was gonna be dog eat dog, eh?

What could *my* angle be?

Maybe I'd appeal to Matt Gates's sympathy? I could explain that I was the product of a broken home, with the world's most wretched sister, plus a set of debilitating allergies. If I didn't win the date, I'd swell up with hives and scratch myself to death.

41

Pathetic, right?

Then came my brainstorm.

Who was head of her debating team in high school?

Who got straight A's in English since first grade?

Carolyn, of course.

If I could trick her into helping me, *she* could be my angle.

I decided to do something totally drastic.

I was going to be nice to my sister!

I started that night at dinner.

It was Carolyn's turn to cook, and she'd made chicken in some slimy sauce with sour cherries. I said it was delicious.

Then I listened as she vomited up her day: how *wonderful* her classes were, how *wonderful* Professor Maxwell was, and how *wonderful* it was to be studying abnormal psychology.

"That's *wonderful*," I said.

That caught her off guard, and she felt obligated to ask about my activities. "Are you still determined to enter that contest at school?"

"Sure."

"Well, I'd advise you not to, Jennifer. You're creating a volatile situation that is bound to end in failure and a feeling of inadequacy. Sometimes accepting one's limitations can actually be a positive action. Producing an essay that would impress Sarah Henley won't be easy. And Matt Gates isn't exactly intellecually inferior either, you know."

Mom seemed surprised. "He isn't?"

"Mother, that comment exhibits reverse sexual prejudice. Just because a man is muscular and handsome, we can't negate the possibility that he might have a brain as well. After all, the name of his group may possibly have deep psychological implications."

This was great! An angle, at last!

"Yeah, real deep," I agreed. "Uh—how, exactly?"

"Well, naturally, it comes from the old adage, 'In the country of the blind, the one-eyed man is king.'"

You could've fooled me. "Yeah, sure, but what's that mean? I mean, of course, I *know*, but I'd like *your* opinion."

"It could have many meanings. It might be a caustic comment on our sociological mores. Or it might be a statement on the mediocrity of popular music in general."

That didn't sound so hot. I could hardly tell Matt Gates I liked his music because it was mediocre!

Carolyn continued. "In a way, these rock groups have now become our cultural icons. They're revered by the juveniles in our society because various mainstays of our Judeo-Christian culture that previously existed are now being eroded."

Yeah, Carolyn was on a roll, and I wished I'd had a pencil. Her psychological mumbo-jumbo was sure to jazz up my essay, if only I could remember it all.

"Correct me if I'm wrong," said Mom, "but aren't you saying that Matt Gate's music is actually garbage?"

"Yes and no. Only in the sense that *all* popular modern literature, art, *and* music is, for the most part, expendable. In this throwaway society, garbage is an attractive commodity because we don't choose to bear the burden of greatness. So in that sense, I think Matt Gates is brilliant."

Terrific. I could see myself writing *that* as a theme: "Dear Matt, Your music is brilliant because it's garbage."

Maybe being nice to Carolyn wouldn't pay off after all. But what other choice did I have? When the phone rang, Carolyn answered it, and I tried to think up some other possibilities, but that led to zero.

"This is awful," said Carolyn, returning to the table. "Professor Maxwell is giving a lecture tonight on negative traits exhibited by subnormal adolescents."

"Then don't go," I suggested.

"I *want* to go, that's the point. I'm sure his theories will enhance my paper, but I'm supposed to sit for Jason at eight. Jennifer, you'll have to fill in for me."

"I don't wanna hear some dumb lecture."

"Not at the lecture, imbecile. Take my place baby-sitting. You promised to be my backup, and you'll make fifteen dollars. Besides, Jason's a brilliant child. You'll have a *wonderful* time."

Why not? I was getting nowhere with my essay. I might as well make some money.

Chapter Six

"How do you do, Jennifer," said Jason Petrie as he answered the door.

I was startled. I mean, for a minute I thought he was a midget or something. "Hi. How'd you know my name?"

"Carolyn called. She's busy. My mommy's busy, too. That's why you're here to sit me."

Mrs. Petrie came out of the bedroom and introduced herself. She was going to a concert, she explained, and would return at eleven. I thought that would be the end of that, but next came a long list of phone numbers: her husband's at work; her pediatrician's; the box office number at Carnegie Hall; and the number of Jason's psychologist, "should he exhibit evidence of anxiety."

Then she ran through the list of Jason's "homework," all to be completed before his bedtime at precisely eight fifteen.

I couldn't believe it! Before the kid could go to sleep, he had to work with math flashcards and listen to the first movement of Beethoven's Third Symphony.

"I know you'll enjoy each other's company," said Mrs. Petrie confidently, then she left.

I smiled at Jason.

Then I stared out the window toward the park. I figured the kid and I could talk awhile and get to know each other.

But Jason stared at me. "We have to work now, Jennifer."

"Oh, sure. What'll we do first?"

"Math, please."

I got out the flashcards and went through a dozen of them. Jason got them all right.

"I can have a snack now," he said. "Then I do my music."

I followed Jason into the kitchen and opened the refrigerator. "What'll it be? Ice cream or cookies?"

"No, I'm not allowed." He pointed to the cupboard. "Crackers."

I took out a box of stone-ground whole wheat thins.

"I can have six," he said, "and a glass of juice."

I poured him a glass of organic papaya juice. "Do you really *like* this stuff?"

"Sure. Want some?"

"No, thanks."

"May I have a napkin, please?"

"A what? Oh yeah."

I gave him a paper napkin. He wiped his mouth, then put his glass in the sink. "I'm ready for my music now."

We went into the living room. Jason put a cassette with a yellow sticker into the stereo, and we both sat down to listen. I don't know much about old Beethoven, but Jason certainly did.

"It's in E flat," he explained, "and it was written for Napoleon."

"No kidding."

"The title means 'heroic.' And that means brave."

"That's nice."

"Here come the winds. And those are the strings."

"You sure know a lot about music."

"Yes, I do. That's the end of the first part. You can turn it off now."

I had a thought. "Now that your homework's finished, maybe you'd like to listen to some other kind of music."

"What kind?"

"More popular stuff." I switched on the radio and turned the dial until I got Matt Gates singing "Snakey Highway," then started dancing to the beat. "Have you ever heard this?"

Jason's eyes lit up. "No. Is this the kind of music you like, Jennifer?"

"Sure, it's great. Don't you think so?"

He grew thoughtful. "It's very loud, isn't it? What's the man saying?"

"I never get all the lyrics, but it's the rhythm that counts."

"Oh."

"Well, how's it make you feel? I really would appreciate your comments."

Okay, if the kid was so smart, maybe *he* could help me. I said I was desperate for an angle!

Jason yawned. "It makes me feel tired. But you can listen. I have to brush my teeth."

As Jason left the room, I realized I'd just hit rockbottom.

I'd actually asked that four-year-old for his advice!

Oh yeah, I had some super chance of winning this contest!

No doubt about it, Jason was years ahead of me, mentally. Carolyn had been right. Getting my hopes up would only mean a bigger disappointment.

I decided to give up.

One of the super A's in English would win the contest—period. After all, this whole idea was just some big-deal publicity stunt to get every girl in the city excited about Matt Gate's new video. Crass commercialism, right? Why should I join in?

I felt relieved after the decision. All the other girls were still running around, ransacking the school library for books on writing techniques while I returned to being happy, sloppy me.

I hoped Carolyn would tell me I'd make a wise decision, but for the next two days all she did was yell. She figured the whole world should stop because she had some sappy psych paper to complete.

"Jam!" she shouted at me as I came home from school. "There's dried-up jam on my books. And my papers, too. What've you been *doing* in this room?"

"Just having a snack."

"You're a pig, Jennifer, an unadulterated pig. I want this entire room reorganized this weekend. I can't continue to live in this sty! Don't make any plans for Saturday, because you're spending it cleaning up."

I made plans anyway.

A bunch of kids were going to the New Yorker theater to see a Steve Martin movie. Chuck was taking Liza. That night, Albert called to ask me to go with him. I hadn't decided about Albert yet, so I accepted.

We were all to meet outside the theater, then go to Charlie's afterward. There were eight of us: Cassie came with her part-time steady, Blake; and our semifriend Christina brought some new guy, Paul.

As we all waited on line, I realized we weren't the only ones with the idea of seeing the movie. Half the kids in school were waiting, too.

Naturally, the hot topic of conversation was the contest. Some of the girls had already finished their essays. Others had made a good start.

I just smiled and kept my mouth shut.

I glanced over at Chuck, who had his arm around Liza. I wasn't certain, but I thought he might be wearing eyeliner.

Anyway, Albert looked real nice. He'd ditched his beat-up jeans and was wearning new ones, with a pretty pastel shirt. I'd seen the same shirt on some guy in a magazine ad, and Albert looked just as good in it. He'd gotten a nice haircut, too.

So Liza didn't know everything. In my opinion, Albert was even better-looking than Chuck.

Well, I really started feeling good. With all those Emerson kids on line, I wasn't at all embarrassed to be seen with Albert. In fact, I was pleased that they were all giving us the eye. (There's always lots of quiet gossip when it seems like a new couple is being launched, and I figured they were all whispering about JennyandAlbert, as if we were the latest item.) Even Liza gave us an envious look.

Yeah, I was feeling good. As we waited on line, boy-girl, boy-girl, down from the corner of Eighty-eighth and Broadway, a funny thought occurred to me. It looked like we were all waiting to file into Noah's ark or something. Everyone had a partner.

I told Albert my Noah's ark theory. Then he told me his theory about people growing to look like their pets.

"You know, Jenny, there's a Great Dane in my building who looks just like his owner. Sometimes when I see them together I can't tell who's who."

I laughed, real loud so everyone could hear me and know I was having a great time.

For a minute, it looked as if Albert and I were the center of attention. But all that suddenly changed when Beryl arrived. Hey, I'm used to Beryl taking the spotlight away from people, but this was ridiculous.

I mean, she didn't arrive like an average ordinary normal person. No, she came on *horseback*.

I'm not kidding.

Naturally, everyone was surprised to see her turning down Broadway on a horse, and naturally everyone stared.

Beryl was wearing the whole outfit: leather boots, riding crop, and britches—even that official riding hat. Most people look like they're hiding a tumor under those things, but on Beryl it looked perfect, especially with her long blond braid bobbing up and down her back.

Of course everyone wanted to know what was up, her being decked out like that.

"I've just come from the Claremont Stables," she announced. "Say hello to Ginger, everyone." Beryl pulled tight on Ginger's reins and sat high in the saddle. She looked like the queen reviewing the Royal Guard or something.

Okay, so the Claremont Stables were only a few blocks away, but it still seemed weird to see Beryl riding horseback up Broadway.

"Ginger and I are off for a little ride," she said. "Anyone want to join us?"

Several kids joked, saying they were fresh out of horses. Then all of a sudden Beryl's horse shook its head and began trotting down the street. Some of the kids commented on what a great "horsewoman" she must be, riding around in traffic like that.

I was glad to see her go. I turned to Albert, hoping to continue our conversation, but he was still staring at Beryl. Her horse had stopped at the corner a moment, then it raised its front legs, shook its head, and began galloping down the street, heading west. I could see Beryl's velvet hat bouncing up and down, as if she were about to jump a hurdle. What a show-off! I was about to say so, too, when Albert cut out of the line and began running down the street. It looked as if he were trying to catch up with her or something.

I couldn't believe it. He actually *chased* Beryl all the way down the street and *jumped on the back of her horse.* He shouted something, then she shouted something, and then they took off.

Together.

All the kids were standing there, staring, as Beryl and Albert galloped away toward Riverside Drive. And once they were out of sight, they all turned around to stare at *me.*

I was totally humiliated.

I mean, this was even worse than being stood up for a date. My date had just been snatched away from me, with half the school for an audience.

"That guy must be nuts about horses," laughed Blake.

"Well, he's nuts about something," Cassie giggled, "or some*one*."

I thought I'd die. As the theater opened and the woman in the booth began taking tickets, I kept wishing I could quietly melt into the cement.

What should I do—Walk away? Make a joke? My feet wouldn't move, and I couldn't think of anything funny, so I just stood there.

"Never mind," said Liza, coming over. "You can sit with us. I told you that guy was strange."

Chuck nudged Liza. I could tell he didn't want me tagging along all afternoon.

"Hey, that's okay," I said, petrified that I might cry, "I'm not in the mood for a movie today." I couldn't have sat in that theater anyway. Everyone would be laughing at me, staring at *me* instead of at the screen.

So I turned around and walked away. I could hear some giggling behind me, but I told myself not to turn around. I didn't want to know which of the group was laughing behind my back.

When I got home, I wrecked my room.

I was so furious, I couldn't stop myself.

I ripped everything out of the drawers and closets, then threw the stuff against the wall. I tore up magazines, envisioning every one as Albert Pierce; but I would've loved to rip *him* into pieces, instead. He was a wimp, a worm, a creep, and I never wanted to see his stinking face again!

Chapter Seven

W ell, it all hit the fan when Carolyn came home.

Expecting to find a cleaned room, she discovered total destruction instead.

"You must be insane!" she screamed. "What came over you?"

I was lying on the bed in a heap (on top of various other heaps I'd thrown there), totally depressed.

"You'll clean this up if it takes all night," she ordered.

I didn't care if it took a lifetime. After all, I could never go back to school again, so I might as well spend my life picking up the pieces.

I was a failure.

A misfit.

A born loser.

No contest, no boyfriend, no hope for the future.

So I started cleaning up.

I mean, *really* cleaning.

Something had snapped in my head, I guess.

As I folded my sweaters, put things back on hangers, and straightened the bookshelves, I tried to plan my future.

I'd hang around the house for a few years, then maybe I'd become a nun. Did convents take non-Catholics? Well, maybe there was some nunnery in a remote corner of the world where they didn't care about religion. A Buddhist temple, maybe. Yeah, high on some Tibetan mountain, where they'd never heard of Albert Pierce—or Matt Gates, for that matter. I could learn to knit or pray or something, somewhere where boys couldn't humiliate me and four-year-olds weren't smarter than I am.

Did such a place exist? Probably not.

I locked the bedroom door, then cleaned some more.

Carolyn banged outside several times, but I didn't let her in.

"You'd better be working in there," she shouted.

I was. My fingers to the bone. I polished. I waxed. I scrubbed. I even decided to put all of Carolyn's sappy papers in order. She had a pile of psychology books scattered around with index cards sticking out.

As I straightened them up, I glanced at her notes. They seemed sort of interesting, so I began to read some. I noticed a whole section about negative traits among sub-normal adolescents. Carolyn had listed several found in feeble-minded individuals:

1. They lack planning capacities.
2. They are irresolute, easily confused.
3. They are silly or obtrusive. Loud or forward.
4. They are simple and suggestible.

5. They have persistent moods, such as foolish elation, obstinacy, and seclusiveness.
6. They are nervous and excitable, overemotional.
7. They are cunning, sly, and deceitful.

Then I read what Carolyn had written following that list. I mean, the words practically bore right through my eyeballs.

"I have found my sister, Jennifer," she wrote, "exhibits *all* of the above tendencies and will therefore be my personal case study to further examine my theory: namely, that prematurity may induce some similarities to feeble-mindedness. My hypothesis is, that Jennifer's premature birth may have disguised or produced an inherent mental or emotional condition, gone undetected and undiagnosed. Naturally, further observations are in order before a decisive conclusion can be made."

I had to read that lousy paragraph twice before I finally got it.

My slimy sister was suggesting *I* was feeble-minded—maybe even subnormal.

I remembered that conversation over dinner about my having been in an incubator. Mom had laughed it off, but Carolyn hadn't been kidding.

I began feeling really strange—not angry at first, just peculiar. When I was little, Mom had always told me I'd come into the world early because I couldn't wait to be part of our family and that's why I was always such a happy baby.

But now I started wondering if there wasn't more to it than that. Could I actually be abnormal because I hadn't waited the regular nine months like everyone else? Was there some important piece of me missing or something?

No. Carolyn was a jerk, and her theory was garbage. If anyone was subnormal in our family, it was Carolyn Leslie Beaumont! And she was using me as a guinea pig to prove her stupid ideas, writing all about it in a paper for everyone at Columbia University to see, announcing to them all that her sister was subnormal.

Then I got angry; I mean, *furious*.

I felt like screaming—a real loud wail that'd get the neighbors calling the police. But it'd probably also get Carolyn running to take more notes.

What an awful feeling. I was under a microscope, being picked at like a bug or a germ or something. I probably hadn't even fooled Carolyn with the makeup business. She *knew* what I'd done to her lipsticks and blush-brushes, and she'd used it as further proof of my cunning and deceit.

I had to get revenge. But wrecking the room again wasn't enough.

How *dare* she think something was wrong with me, anyhow?

I'd show the world I wasn't subnormal, that I could achieve, win, succeed, just like anyone else.

But how?

Well, the answer wasn't too far away. As I shoved those disgusting notes back into the book, I noticed Carolyn's term paper lying on the desk with a fat red A+ scrawled on it. It was that big-deal essay she'd been bragging about for days and about which I'd personally been too bored to listen: "The Ramifications of the Beatles on a Generation."

As I glanced through it, a truly cunning, sly, deceitful,

brilliant thought hit me. With a few minor changes, it could easily qualify for the contest, as "What Your Music Means to Me."

Easily.

I mean, it was perfect. All I'd have to do was change most of the references from the Beatles to Country of the Blind—make Ringo into Bryan, etc., etc.

Yeah, it'd be sure to win.

I read through the entire paper, then began copying it over, with a few deletions. Actually, lots of the stuff was a little pompous and barfy, but who cared? Some of the closing lines nearly made me gag, but I wrote them anyway: "As Mary Cassatt once commented [said Carolyn], 'Success on other people's terms is no achievement at all.'"

I didn't exactly know what that meant. I wasn't even sure who Mary Cassatt was, or if she'd ever met a rock group. But it'd probably impress Sarah Henley, anyway.

Yeah, things were looking up.

I told myself it wasn't cheating, just poetic justice. If Carolyn could pick my brain, I could pick hers, too. I mean, fair is fair, right?

I'd get that date with Matt Gates, become the star of Emerson High, and make Albert Pierce sorry he ditched me!

Chapter Eight

Albert called six times that night, but I refused to speak to him. Mom kept taking messages, but I kept throwing them away.

Sunday, I spent the whole afternoon typing up my essay from the written notes I'd stolen.

Carolyn couldn't figure out what was up. The room was clean, and I was *working*. Well, let her wonder. Let her sneak around, writing down "tendencies." My revenge was already in progress.

Early Monday morning, I delivered my cleanly typed essay into Sarah Henley's hands.

She seemed startled. "Goodness, Jennifer, it's fifteen pages. Most other girls only handed in four or five."

"Yeah, well, I had a lot to say."

She glanced over the first page. "Undoubtedly. It seems quite well thought out, too."

"Yeah, I was inspired."

"I'm delighted. I was afraid this contest might intimidate some of our, well, less literary students. But now I see it's unleashed all sorts of dormant feelings in you girls."

"Yeah, all sorts." (If old Henley only knew!)

"Well, I'm glad of that. As I've said to all the girls, good luck. And may the best essay win. This is quite a responsibility for me, you know."

I sure hoped Henley knew her business. If she couldn't pick out an A college student's paper from a bunch of high-school kids', she was even dottier than I supposed.

At dinner that night, I told Mom I'd entered the contest.

"Well, let's see your essay. I'd love to read it."

"*Read* it? Oh no, you can't."

"Why not?"

Good question—one I'd have to think up a lie for, fast.

"Well, I don't have a carbon, and the original is the property of the record company. Anyway, all us kids had to sign releases, saying we'd never show what we wrote to another living soul."

"That's ridiculous," said Carolyn. "What kind of idiotic rule is that?"

"I don't know. I guess that's show business!"

Later that night, Albert called again. I'd avoided him during lunch. I'd avoided everyone. I knew every kid in school must still be laughing their heads off over the fool he'd made of me on Saturday.

But why was he still calling? He'd already dumped me in full view of everyone.

I called Liza for advice.

"Maybe he wants to apologize," she suggested. "If I were you, I'd be curious to hear the excuse he comes up with."

"No excuse could be good enough. He made a fool of me."

"Maybe so," she agreed, "but why let him know it? If you don't take his calls, he'll know you feel terrible."

"Well, I do. I practically *ran* through the lunchroom today, hoping no one would stop to ask me about him."

"So don't let him know that. Pretend it meant nothing; that's what I'd do."

When Albert called an hour later, I decided to talk to him.

"Look, Jenny, I know you must be furious with me."

"Furious? What about?"

"Saturday, naturally."

I tried taking Liza's advice and acted casual. "Oh— Saturday. Hey, that's okay. The gang said it was a sappy movie anyhow."

"Really? Well, you must've thought I was a jerk, taking off on that horse like that."

I didn't tell him what I really thought. To me, he'd looked just like Indiana Jones galloping down the street.

"Yeah, you did look stupid."

"I'll bet. I suppose the kids from school thought I was nuts."

Was it possible he didn't know? Since the incident, some of the girls had started calling him Mr. Macho Man. "I wouldn't know; I've been busy."

"Oh. Well, I thought I'd call and explain. See, I've been riding horses since I was six, so I could tell Beryl didn't know what she was doing. Did you notice her feet? They were in the stirrups all wrong, and she was holding her reins too tight. Her thumbs were in the wrong position, too."

"Is that a fact?"

"Sure. Those horses are trained to walk or trot right into Central Park. They canter sometimes, but never gallop, not unless the rider is out of control. And they *never* go down Broadway, because the traffic frightens them. Beryl would've taken that horse straight down Riverside Drive and onto the West Side Highway if I hadn't stopped her. She might've gotten killed."

Was it true? Was Albert trying to save Beryl's life, not make a date with her? I wanted to believe that, but knew I shouldn't sound too eager about it.

"That was nice of you, Albert. I hope she thanked you."

"Not really."

"Well, let's forget the whole thing, okay? It really wasn't important. I'm free on Sunday, if you want to try again."

"No, not Sunday. I couldn't see you Sunday!"

Uh-oh, I'd blown it. I'd sounded *too* eager. "Oh. Well, let's skip it altogether then, okay? I forgot, I'm busy on Sunday, too."

I couldn't wait to hang up.

"You're kidding," said Liza, when she called me later. "He actually said he was trying to *save her life?*"

"Not in those words, but that's the idea."

"You didn't believe him, did you?"

"What do *you* think?"

"Well, I suppose it could be true. Anything's possible. But my guess is, Albert thought he had a great come-on to catch Beryl's attention. She probably told him to get lost, so now he's trying to get back with you."

"Then why'd he turn me down for Sunday?"

"Maybe he *does* have a date with Beryl, but he wants to string you along on the side."

"That worm! Well, it won't work. Once I win the contest, I'll have my pick of guys, anyway."

"*Win?* I thought you'd given up."

"No, I gave Henley my essay this morning."

Liza didn't say anything.

"Are you still there?" I asked.

"Sure. What made you change your mind? You must've come up with some pretty terrific angle. What is it?"

"That's *my* secret. Dog eat dog, remember?"

Chapter Nine

For the next week, a lottery atmosphere took over Emerson High as Matt Gates mania grew.

Lots of guys in school with their own little bands started making tapes to dump on Country of the Blind when they came to school. Yeah, amateur musicians came crawling from out of the woodwork. And Mrs. Henley said she'd received a "large degree of superior work that would be challenging to assess" and that she'd had "difficulty with various nomenclature."

Nomenclature?

"That means she's never heard of funk or punk," said Liza.

"Oh."

Well, I hoped Carolyn's essay wouldn't be over her head, too!

An official Decorating Committee was formed to jazz up the auditorium for the big day, namely May seventeenth, when Matt Gates and the band would appear in person to greet the lucky winner.

There were articles in the paper and spots on the local news about it—which caused lots of trouble for Emerson High. Mr. Corbett arranged to hire extra security guards for that day, after word got out that kids from other schools planned to crash. Lots of PCS kids (usually they were above it all) threatened to charge over with their eight-by-ten glossies.

Even the mayor seemed worried. On television he announced that a special police escort would accompany the group. Matt Gates's idea to get a ton of free publicity from this contest was really paying off.

I mean, Emerson began turning into Russia. All of us were issued ID cards so no intruders could infiltrate.

Most of the kids loved all the excitement, but some of the teachers looked as if they might fall apart, especially Sarah Henley. Having to pick a winner was hard enough, but when she found out who Country of the Blind actually were—well, it came as a shock.

We were hanging up the group's posters in the auditorium when she came in. There's this one really great shot of Matt in black leather jeans and nothing else, except his silver cord, of course. I could tell old Henley thought it was objectionable.

"*This* is the young man who initiated the contest?"

Poor old Henley. I hoped she wouldn't go bonkers before she picked a winner.

At home, Carolyn was in shock, too. She couldn't believe I'd actually entered the competition and that I hoped to *win*. Whenever she could, she made nasty psychological comments about my "delusions of grandeur overcompensating as a defense mechanism"—junky stuff like that.

Even Mom got annoyed. "Don't you want your sister to win?"

"That's not the point, Mother. Jennifer's failure is inevitable. I'm merely advising her to be realistic."

I *was* getting nervous. The big day was rapidly approaching, and it'd become more important than ever that I win. Sure, the popularity and fame would be great, but I also wanted to shut my sister's big fat mouth forever. Carolyn would have to tear up all her half-baked theories and would hopefully wind up with a Z in psychology.

Then my revenge would be complete.

By May fifteenth, I was a nervous wreck. In my case, that meant that every allergy hiding in my body had suddenly decided to pop out. My eyes watered, my feet itched, and as for my sinuses, they'd gone beserk. They were so clogged up, only Drano could've unplugged them.

I lay awake all night, starting the countdown. The next day, the winner would be announced. The day after, Country of the Blind would come to school. That following Saturday, May twenty-fifth, the big Dream Date was scheduled, after which, the world would never be the same—for someone.

Would it be me?

As I lay in the dark, I got a fantastic thought. If I won, I could write another essay and sell it to *Seventeen* magazine: "My Dream Date With Matt Gates." Every girl in the country would want to read it, right?

Yeah, it *had* to be me.

Somewhere around two A.M., I got up to check my horoscope. There's this great magazine that gives a daily blow-by-blow description for each sign. I looked up Pisces, May sixteenth: "If you travel today, drive with care..."

That was a big help!

But the next morning on my way to school, I began wondering if the bus driver was a Pisces, too. Maybe he'd crash before I discovered if I'd won?

I tell you, I was a wreck.

I didn't think I'd last until three P.M.

None of us did. During lunch, everyone had just one topic of conversation. Lots of us tried cornering Henley after each period, hoping she'd leak some clue about the winner.

She was silent as a tomb. "All shall be revealed after classes, girls. Be patient."

Well, at three o'clock, we all piled into the auditorium to hear the verdict. I noticed Veronica Patterson looking superconfident. Veronica's a senior with a scholarship to Vassar in the fall and an inflated vocabulary only matched by her inflated ego.

I could tell she thought she'd won.

In fact, *all* the seniors seemed to think they'd won.

I said a silent prayer that Carolyn was the hotshot writer that she seemed to think she was.

Mr. Corbett called for order, then introduced Mrs. Henley and Mr. Banks (as if we didn't know them by now).

"I assume you all know why we're here," he joked.

No one laughed.

"Yes, well, Mrs. Henley informs me she's received a number of truly fine essays."

"That's quite right," Mrs. Henley agreed. "I was happily surprised at the plethora of talent within our ranks. Unfortunately, some of the musical phraseology was foreign to me, but Mr. Banks assures me that many of you young ladies have a wide musical knowledge."

Liza poked me. "I told you that technical stuff would impress her."

Minutes dragged on like hours as Henley went on about how great all the essays were, how hard it had been to decide, how difficult it had been to select one, and how challenging the whole thing was for everyone.

"...But in the final analysis, there are only three criteria one must use in the selection of a winning essay. Namely: style, content, and composition. To achieve a perfect score on all these is always the goal of a truly fine essayist. Now, addressing myself to the first point, one mustn't confuse style with mere rhetoric, as is often the case..."

Like I said, on and on.

My legs started itching.

Hello, hives!

I could feel them popping out as I scraped my feet against the floor and wiggled my toes inside my sneakers.

But Henley showed no mercy. She had a captive audience for her loony speech, and she didn't care that we only wanted to hear the name of the winner.

"...which led me to the inevitable choice of Jennifer Beaumont."

I was bent over my seat, scratching inside my socks.

Had Henley called my name?

"Who?" lots of kids called out (including me).

"Yes, Jennifer Beaumont is the winner. Such quality work from a freshman is quite rare."

The next few minutes seemed like a fuzzy dream. Liza started pushing me toward the stage, and I could hear voices behind me.

"Jennifer Beaumont? Who's *that?*"

"*Jenny?* You're kidding!"

"Not *Beaumont;* no way!"

"*Who?*"

Well, at least they were all saying my name, so it must be me.

Standing by the podium, Mrs. Henley was gesturing me toward her. "Congratulations, dear; well done."

I think I stood there for a minute halfway between the stage and the seats, gazing out at everyone. I noticed various faces in the crowd. Veronica looked real surprised; so did Cassie; so did Liza. Everyone did.

"I'm sure this warrants your applause," coaxed Mrs. Henley.

None of the kids seemed to agree, but they began clapping anyway.

It made me feel really creepy.

For a second, I was tempted to confess everything. Well, not *everything.* I couldn't admit that I'd stolen the winning essay, but I could be gracious and say my sister had helped by her inspiration.

Luckily, the feeling quickly passed. No one expected me to make a speech anyway, so I didn't.

It was now official. I'd won.

So it really didn't matter how I'd done it, right?

"I'm glad it was you," Liza reassured me, going home. "If it couldn't be me, then I'm glad it's my best friend. Boy, you must've worked like a demon, Jen. I can't believe you beat out all those seniors. Did you see Veronica's face? I thought she'd die!"

Albert called that evening.

"Congratulations, Jenny. I wanted to say that at school, but there was such a crowd. I was hoping you'd win. I want you to know that, okay?"

Mom was thrilled. She called Dad in Seattle, and he called me back late that night to wish me luck on my big date.

"I bet there'll be something in the newspaper about it. So clip it out and send it to me—don't forget."

Carolyn actually said she was *proud* of me.

Stunned, but proud.

"I didn't think you could do it, but if Mrs. Henley chose your essay, it must've been the best. I guess your determination paid off, Jennifer."

That night, as I lay in bed, I didn't feel so hot.

Was this a conspiracy or what?

Why was everyone being such a good sport in this deal?

How come no one—especially Carolyn—had gotten the idea I might've cheated to win?

Then a scary thought hit me. Maybe it wasn't just an idea. What if Carolyn *knew* I'd cheated—just like she'd known about the lipsticks and blush brushes and everything? But she hadn't known about those things—or had she?

Well, maybe she was biding her time, taking notes, just waiting for me to crack. Psychological warfare, I think it's called. I bet Carolyn knew all about that. Sure, I was the enemy, and she was lulling me into some false sense of security, just waiting for the proper time to pull the rug out from under me.

As I lay in the dark, I could hear the clock ticking away beside my bed, ticking off the minutes, until Carolyn came rushing in, shouting, *"I know what you did!"*

But Carolyn didn't come in.

Around midnight, I couldn't stand that tick-tock any longer, so I shoved the clock under my pillow and got up for some milk. Mom was still in the living room doing homework. Carolyn wasn't even home. Mom said she was baby-sitting for Jason.

So maybe I was wrong. Carolyn didn't know anything; no one did. Still, I couldn't shake that panicky feeling.

I guess fear can't keep you awake forever, though. I mean, we all go through life knowing we're going to die someday, but we don't spend every minute worrying about it, right?

Around two o'clock, I finally fell asleep.

Chapter Ten

Next morning, the outside of school looked like a zoo: a total mess, a real disaster area.

I mean, I'd no idea!

First off, there were rows of cars (lots of them limos), a film van, and two patrol cars parked along the block. The cops also had put up barriers against the sidewalk.

At least half the teen-agers in the city must've cut classes to stand outside Emerson, all screaming and waving banners and albums.

Teachers were adding to the confusion by shouting for kids to be orderly. No way!

The security guards were trying to check ID's, but no one wanted to enter school, knowing they'd miss Country of the Blind's arrival. So hundreds of kids piled up along the street, making it impossible to tell the Emerson students from the truants.

Mr. Corbett rallied everyone into action, including Jack

Katz, the gym teacher. Katz was standing on the street, blowing his whistle, which naturally no one heard.

I quickly gave up thoughts of strolling into school as the center of attention. Forget it. I was lucky I didn't get trampled.

Everyone was pushing and shouting like mad.

"Which limo is theirs?"

"Can you see them yet?"

"Is this gonna be on television?"

Then a rumor started to circulate that, to throw everyone off the scent, the group was arriving in a taxi. No taxis pulled up, but pretty soon people started exiting from one of the limos. There was an old guy with a beard, two lady-executive types, and a fat man in a three-piece suit. They began talking to Mr. Corbett by the steps of school, giving him lots of instructions. After that, two men in jeans jumped from back of the van, carrying hand-held cameras. They started shouting for the crowd to be pushed back, so four policemen jumped from patrol cars and began shoving. Then some more cops formed a human chain outside the school entrance. Finally, Country of the Blind snuck out from another limo, which was the third in line.

At least, I think it was them. They were all wearing their concert-entrance outfits—long black leather capes, large black felt hats, and huge sunglasses—so it was hard to be sure. As they made a dash for the entrance, the cameras rolled and the crowd tried to break through the police barriers.

I mean, if you'd blinked, you would've missed them, they ran so fast. It reminded me of those old silent movies where everything is speeded up.

Once the group was safely inside, Mr. Corbett started forming all the Emerson kids in lines so the guards could look at ID's. Then, single file, we were all herded into the auditorium.

I personally got stepped on several times.

Someone said three kids who were trying to crash the line had fainted in the street, so the school nurse rushed outside with her first aid kit.

By this time, Mr. Corbett looked as if he were having a coronary. "Don't worry," he kept assuring the frazzled teachers, who'd given up trying to keep control, "I think things are going well, don't you?" Then he gave us that line about our all being "mature young ladies and gentlemen" and how proud he was of us. I guess he hadn't noticed half the school banging on the seats and chanting "Bring on the Blind, bring on the Blind."

By now, Mr. Three-Piece Suit was standing onstage. "Okay, kids, calm down. We've got a tight schedule to keep here. Matt Gates and the band are catching a plane at noon, so let's begin. My name is Sidney Whitehead, president of Sandpiper Records, and I'd like to tell you our plans for the morning. There'll be a forty-five-minute autograph session, one album per student. Details of the May twenty-fifth date will be furnished to your principal by the end of the week. So now let's meet the lucky young lady who won the prize: an all-expense-paid date with you-know-who. Will she come up onstage, please?"

My big moment had arrived. Unfortunately, I was stuck in the middle of a row and had to step over eight pairs of feet to get to the aisle. Somehow I made it through, and Mrs. Henley escorted me onto the stage. She was tugging at some papers that were probably a sappy speech she'd prepared about how the winner had been chosen. She was about to read it when Mr. Whitehead said there wasn't time, so we were spared.

By now, all the kids were again shouting "Bring on the Blind" at the top of their voices.

Suddenly, the guests of honor appeared from behind the curtain, still in their long capes, hats, and glasses. Those four shadowy figures in black sure caused a riot, even though no one could actually *see* them. For all I knew, they were four impostors, disguised as Country of the Blind. I mean, they didn't even take off their glasses. Well, maybe they thought they'd be attacked (which was probably right).

Yeah, everyone went berserk.

One of the group—I suppose it was Matt—walked over to shake my hand and take me toward the microphone.

"Thatta girl, love," he whispered.

That English accent certainly sounded like Matt. And he'd called me "love." I hoped all the kids heard *that!*

No one heard anything. The mike wasn't on. By the time everyone realized the problem, there was no point in fixing it, because the "presentation" part of the big event was over.

The two female execs began dragging tables and chairs onto the stage, and Mr. Banks announced that the autographing session would begin.

As kids stampeded down the aisles with their albums, a lot of them broke the line and jumped onstage, so I nearly got trampled again.

I hadn't thought to bring my album, so I didn't even get an autograph.

Several piggy kids tried getting in line more than once.

So did some of the teachers, who were supposed to be keeping order.

I mean, the whole thing was like some crazed assembly line. Country of the Blind was seated in a row, each scrawling his name in fast motion on an album. With those spy outfits on, I really couldn't tell which one was Tom or Rick or Bryan or Matt.

The whole thing was over before I knew what hit me. As a matter of fact, something *did* hit me. When Mr. Whitehead announced the autograph session was over, some kid on back of the line threw an album up front, which got me in the eye.

Then the policemen who'd been waiting outside hurried down the aisle to escort the group back to the waiting limousine. We could hear the sirens screeching as Matt Gates and his band were raced toward the airport.

It was over.

Kids started leaving the auditorium and going back to official classes.

Liza ran up to me in the hall, breathless. "Wasn't it wonderful? Bryan signed my album. Look, he wrote, 'To my fan, from Bryan Hall.' Isn't that something?"

I was still in a daze.

"Did you see their wild outfits?" She sighed. "I thought they only wore those things in concert. Oh, and I actually touched Rick's arm. I just leaned over and touched it. What's the matter with you, Jen? You don't seem at all excited."

"Well, everything happened so fast."

"Yeah, sure, but celebrities have tight schedules. They're probably flying to the coast to make some wild new video or something. But at least we *saw* them. Anyway, what'd you expect?"

I didn't dare tell Liza what I'd expected; it'd sound too silly. I had figured that when Matt Gates saw me coming onstage, he'd at least take off his glasses. I mean, I longed to know what color his eyes were. Then he could've slowly walked toward me as we both made eye contact: something like those slow-motion deals in the deodorant commercials. He'd take my hand and say he was really looking forward to our date, and that I was the prettiest girl he'd ever seen.

"Well," Liza repeated, "what *did* you expect?"

"Nothing, I guess. It was just fast, that's all."

"Look who's complaining. All we have is autographs. Next week, you'll actually *be* with Matt Gates. Where do you suppose he'll take you? To some romantic, dimly lit spot, do you suppose? He's so rich, maybe he has a yacht. Wouldn't that be great—dinner on his yacht? Oh, Jenny, you must be so excited!"

Well, maybe I would be. But so far, things weren't working out as I'd planned. After all, this was supposed to be my day, too, right? I'd won the contest. Matt Gates had come to see *me*, hadn't he?

So far, all I had to show for it was one sore eye that I sincerely hoped wouldn't turn black and blue.

If this was fame, you could've fooled me.

But Liza was right. My big date was coming up. Then everything would be different.

After I'd spent an evening with Matt Gates, kids would notice me for sure!

The next day, Mom received a special delivery letter from Sidney Whitehead at Sandpiper Records.

76

Dear Mrs. Beaumont:

Following are the details of your daughter's date with Matt Gates on Saturday, May 25th. She will be picked up by a Sandpiper representative at 7 o'clock and escorted to La Maison Rouge restaurant. After dinner, there will be a pleasant interlude at Pogo's, where dancing and entertainment will be provided. After this, your daughter will be accompanied home at precisely 10 o'clock.

I'm sure your daughter will enjoy this chaperoned evening out with one of the music industry's most dynamic celebrities.

No other family members may attend.

Sincerely yours,

Sidney Whitehead

Mom thought it was all terribly impressive.

I didn't. I mean, my name wasn't even mentioned in the letter. Matt Gates still didn't know who I was.

"Well dear, I guess you can't expect a personal note from Mr. Gates."

"But he's not even coming to pick me up."

"Of course not; you'll be suitably chaperoned the entire evening. I wouldn't let you go otherwise."

So much for candlelight and yachts!

Later that night, Albert called.

"How're you doing? I saw that album come flying at your face at assembly."

Why was he mentioning *that*? "I'm fine."

"That's good. I don't know much about rock music, but

the whole deal seemed like a lot of fuss over nothing. Those guys didn't have much going for them except their English accents."

Why was he being so nasty? "Is that what you called to tell me?"

"No. There's a biology test tomorrow. I figured you'd need help studying."

And why was he always making out I was stupid? "I don't need any help, thanks. I'll pass; no problem."

Of course, I failed the biology test.

But my mind was on more important things, namely, how could I look ravishingly beautiful by Saturday night? Money would help, but I couldn't afford a new outfit, and I was still paying Mom back the money I owed Carolyn. I couldn't ask her to advance me any more, not after I brought home my report card. Biology wasn't the only disaster area: I flunked almost everything.

"I can't understand it," said Mom. "How could you do so well on your essay, yet get a sixty-five in English?"

English was one of my *good* marks. "Well, at least I didn't fail."

The minute Carolyn got wind of my report card, I thought I was in big trouble. It would only take her a second to put two and two together and realize I hadn't written that winning essay. Once she'd figured that part out, could the rest be far behind? How long would it take her to remember her essay sitting in our room?

I held my breath and waited. But Carolyn didn't say a word, at least nothing terrible. She stared at my report card and kept repeating "Very interesting," then went running to her psych books.

All I could figure was that she was extending her "water torture" treatment until dinner.

Dinner came and went; still no word. As I washed up the dishes, I again had visions of her bursting through the kitchen door shouting *I know what you did!* I'd heard those words so often in my mind, but so far she hadn't said them. I prayed for some sign that would let me know just when it'd happen.

But the next day, something great happened, instead. Dad sent me a telegram saying KNOCK HIM DEAD ON SATURDAY. In it was a money order for one hundred dollars. All for me. My clothing problems were solved.

And things started picking up at school, too. Barney Weston, editor of the school paper, wanted to interview me about my winning essay. All the girls had a crush on Barney. It was highly publicized that he liked "older women" and only went out with college girls.

Then Beryl asked me to sit at her table. She wanted to know all about my plans for the big date: what I was going to wear, what kind of makeup, everything. She even offered to go shopping with me that Saturday.

"I know some great places downtown where they sell designer clothes at discount. All the models go there."

That part was sticky, since Liza had already offered to shop with me at Bloomingdale's. What to do? I decided to accept Beryl's offer. After all, it wasn't the principle, but the money. Liza would understand.

But Liza seemed annoyed. "Jenny, it was all planned. I looked through Bloomie's catalog last night and circled lots of things for you. And I was going to help with your makeup, remember?"

"That's okay, Beryl's offered to do that, too. She's got

hundreds of samples and a million blush brushes."

"I see. You two've gotten real chummy, haven't you?"

"Well, you were right. Beryl's not so bad, once you get to know her."

"Thanks for telling me."

As you can see, things were going great at school. But by the time I got home, I was in a panic again, figuring Carolyn had finally found me out. How much longer would it take for her to realize the truth? I couldn't hold up much longer.

But then I overheard her talking on the phone to her boyfriend, John.

"I'm taking a new approach on my paper. I might investigate the savant syndrome. You know, deficient people can often excel in one particular area; in fact, it's quite common. I've read about a man who didn't learn to walk until he was thirty, yet he could play anything on the piano after hearing it only once. No, John, of course I'm not suggesting Jennifer is an *idiot*. I merely think I've found the explanation for her winning essay. You must admit it's very interesting from a psychological point of view. After all, great behavioral theories have been formed from the discovery of tiny personality quirks. I've just read another fascinating study by Professor..."

I didn't need to listen any longer. I was off the hook!

My sappy sister figured it all had something to do with her sappy theory about me. The next day, she went running back to the library to collect a mess more books. This time, they were all about wolf children and dual personalities.

Yeah, things were finally going my way.

At school on Thursday, I was the center of attention at

Beryl's table. The spotlight had finally been turned on me, and I was enjoying every second.

Barney Weston said he was setting aside a whole page of the school paper for his exclusive interview with me.

Friday, I cut school. I told Mom it was sinus trouble, but I really had an appointment for a haircut and facial.

By now, I was feeling like an athlete revving up for the big race.

Nothing could stop me now!

Chapter Eleven

The next day, Beryl took me on my shopping spree.

We went to four discount houses downtown, which for me was a real experience. I mean, I'd never shopped like that before—in back rooms, showrooms, and literally off the rack. At first, I thought there was something illegal about it, the prices seemed so cheap.

"Don't be silly," said Beryl. "These are the true prices, before the department stores add their markup."

Well, I tried on dozens of dresses, looking for the perfect one. At the fourth place, I finally decided on a pale blue silk with millions of tiny pleats. I thought it'd be great for dancing, and it was a real bargain.

Beryl approved. "Matt Gates's favorite color is blue. I read that in *Rolling Stone*."

Next, Beryl helped me pick out shoes (pale blue satin heels) and a pair of long rhinestone earrings. When we were finished, we stopped for sodas.

"I read something else about Matt Gates," said Beryl.

"That magazine said he likes younger girls."

"How young?"

"Well, maybe not as young as us, but who knows. Life is full of surprises."

Since Beryl was being so chummy, I couldn't resist asking what I was dying to know. "Tell me something. What do you think of Albert Pierce?"

"He's okay. He made me feel like a jerk the other day, but he's all right."

"I heard the two of you were seeing each other. This Sunday, right?"

"Me and Albert? No way. Oh, I suppose he's cute in a rustic way, but he's never asked me out or anything. Most boys don't anymore."

"Quit kidding. You've always got tons of guys hanging around."

"Sure. They hang around and stare, but they never ask me for a date."

"Why not?"

"I suppose they think I'm going to turn them down, now that I'm a model. They may think I have heavy dates every night, but that's ridiculous. When I model after school, I have to be in bed by nine. Anyway, whatever the reason, they don't call me."

"Not even Albert?"

"No. Why are we talking about Albert, anyway? Matt Gates is far more interesting. Say, we'd better get moving and start on your makeup. I've learned some great cosmetic secrets that I can try out on you. You've got real good bone structure, Jenny. When I'm finished, you'll look at least eighteen."

"Listen, why are you doing all this for me?"

"Why? To be nice, I guess. Besides, it's fun. When I first started modeling, lots of girls at the agency helped me out, too. Of course, I'd much rather be dating Matt Gates myself, but I'm such a rotten English student. C'mon, let's get home and make you gorgeous for tonight."

A major attack of the guilties was creeping up on me again. I felt lousy, knowing Beryl *was* nice, once you got to know her.

By six o'clock, I was transformed. I felt like a character in an old movie who's had plastic surgery, but the doctors won't let her look at her new face when the bandages come off. I was dying to get to the mirror, but Beryl kept adding one more finishing touch. She used so many different shades and kinds of makeup, my face felt like an artist's canvas.

"Don't worry." She smiled. "Everything is hypo-allergenic. My skin's sensitive, too, so I know your problem."

When she finally allowed me to look at myself, I couldn't believe it. My face was fantastic. A masterpiece! No kidding, it was like one of those beauty makeovers in the magazines.

Beryl liked my new hairdo but said it wasn't sophisticated enough, so she pulled part of it back and let little wisps fall from the sides. "That's much more dramatic with those earrings, Jenny."

While I got dressed, Beryl continued to fuss over me like my fairy godmother. "Blue's really your color, Jenny. It brightens up your eyes. The first thing a girl should do is find her colors, then stick with them. It makes life so much easier."

When we were finished, Liza stopped by to see the end results. "Jenny, you look great. That dress is much nicer than the ones I saw in the Bloomie's catalog. And your makeup's fantastic!"

"Are you sure? But I feel so nervous."

"Of course you're nervous, stupid. You're dating Matt Gates!"

It was more than that. I couldn't help thinking that the fairy-tale part of this deal couldn't last forever. Pretty soon the pumpkin part would be coming up. Was it just those guilties again? Maybe so.

Carolyn wasn't around to see my grand entrance, but Mom was waiting anxiously in the hallway for the great unveiling.

She smiled and said one word: "Perfect."

Our doorbell rang at seven P.M. precisely. I took one final look at myself, then ran to answer it.

It was the bearded man I'd seen at school with Country of the Blind. He introduced himself as Douglas Fieldstone and said he was the group's personal manager and that he'd be escorting me to the restaurant. "Which one of you is Jennifer?"

"That's me."

"Well, it looks like you're all set to roll, right, Jennifer? Good, because the camera crew is all set to roll, too. They're waiting at La Maison Rouge for our arrival."

"Cameras?" asked Mom. "What for?"

"There've been some last-minute changes, Mrs. Beaumont. Matt came up with a great new idea. He's thinking of incorporating some of this Dream Date stuff into his new video. He hopes to write a whole new song around it."

Liza couldn't believe it. "You mean Jenny might wind up on MTV?"

"It's possible. Let's see how things go. Of course, that would mean legal releases from you, Jennifer. It would also mean money, naturally."

"And fame?" squealed Liza.

"Yes, that's possible, too."

"What'd I tell you?" said Beryl. "Life's full of surprises, just like I said."

I felt I must be dreaming. "You mean I might get *paid* for dating Matt Gates?"

Mr. Fieldstone laughed. "Yes, quite well, if things work out as planned. So just relax and be natural this evening. Matt likes everything honest and natural. The whole idea is for you to enjoy yourself while you're out with a famous celebrity."

How could I help it!

Mr. Fieldstone checked his watch. "Well, time is money, so we'd better keep on schedule. Don't worry, Mrs. Beaumont, we'll take good care of your daughter this evening. Sandpiper Records will give her a great night on the town and something to put in her memory book. Well, our limo is waiting."

"A limousine? Waiting for me?"

"Naturally. When you date Matt Gates, you go in style."

If I'd had time, I would've pinched myself. But before I knew it, Mr. Fieldstone had whisked me out of the door and into the waiting limousine.

Now I felt even better than Cinderella.

I felt like a queen!

Chapter Twelve

My entrance into La Maison Rouge can only be described in one word: spectacular.

A uniformed doorman wearing epaulettes greeted me as I got out of the limousine, and he escorted me through the brass-filigreed entranceway.

I took Mr. Fieldstone's arm as the headwaiter graciously smiled at me. "Good evening, Mademoiselle Beaumont. Everything has been prepared for your pleasure."

Mademoiselle. My pleasure. I'd never *heard* stuff like that before!

And naturally, I'd never been in such a fancy place before. Crystal chandeliers dripped from the ceiling, and the linen-covered tables had huge bowls of fresh flowers and silver candlesticks. Oil paintings hung on the brocaded walls, which made the place look more like a palace than a restaurant. Violinists playing romantic music strolled among the tables, and the sound of their strings mingled with the clinking of people's crystal glasses.

"Your party is assembled in the private dining room," explained the waiter, opening two large oak doors and ushering us inside.

There, four camermen greeted my arrival. As the film began to roll, I gasped.

"Great reaction shot," shouted one of the crew.

Well, my reaction was genuine. I hadn't thought it possible, but this room was even fancier than the main dining room. It had gilded cupids hanging from the walls and a grand piano inlaid with mother-of-pearl in the corner. A pianist dressed in a white tuxedo was playing a dreamy melody. This place was definitely a step up from Charlie's!

In the center of the room, a large lace-covered table was already set, with several people seated around it. I recognized the two lady execs I'd seen before, and Mr. Whitehead, president of the record company. Mr. Fieldstone introduced me to them, as well as several other recording and video executives. Everyone said I looked "charming" and was happy I'd won the contest—junk like that.

But I didn't see Matt Gates. The waiter seated me at the head of the table, while the camera crew kept running around taking shots of me from different angles.

"She looks great, don't you think?" one of them shouted.

"Perfect," said another. "Innocence, plus charm."

The whole thing seemed more like a dream. But the dreamiest part came when Matt Gates arrived. He came walking through the doorway, dressed in white, like he'd just dropped from a cloud. He was wearing a creamy white cashmere sweater and slacks with a black satin bow tie casually clipped to the center of the silver cord around his neck. His soft curly brown hair glistened, but best of all, he wasn't wearing sunglasses.

I mean, it was awesome. I, Jennifer Beaumont, was actually staring into Matt Gates's eyes. They were large and green—like the ocean, like emeralds, like a forest. I mean, *green*. And he was definitely the most gorgeous hunk on earth.

As he walked toward me, I grew weak in the knees (which was okay, because I was sitting down). He leaned over, took my hand, then kissed it. "Hello, love, you look charming."

It was all over in a second, but my cheeks burned hot for several minutes. As my head cleared, Matt sat down next to me and the waiter placed shrimp cocktails in front of us. They were the biggest shrimp I'd ever seen! I stared at the shrimp, then stared at the hand Matt Gates had kissed. It still looked the same, but I knew it never would be.

Everyone at the table began eating, but I couldn't seem to swallow. Lots of them asked me questions: how old I was, how long I'd been a Matt Gates fan, what my favorite song was, and so on. I must've answered them, but I don't remember what I said. I guess I was still drooling over Matt Gates. He was so close, I could feel his breath. So close, I could *die*.

But I managed to catch some of the conversation. Mr. Fieldstone kept telling me to be myself, and Mr. Whitehead explained they weren't taping our conversation, just the visuals, so I shouldn't be embarrassed. Mr. Abernathy, the president of Video Visuals, said he was real excited about filming at Pogo's later on. "The lush splendor of La Maison Rouge will be a sharp contrast to the funky atmosphere of Pogo's. And that's just what we're reaching for here—a culture shock contrast, with this little lady thrown into the middle of it all."

I heard all the words, but most didn't make much sense. I had to keep reminding myself that I was the "little lady" they kept talking about.

Matt Gates didn't say anything. When the main course arrived, the waiter explained it was called Oiseau sans Têtes. Translating, he said that meant "birds without heads." Actually, they weren't birds at all, but strips of beef rolled around something, and they smelled delicious.

As I tried tasting one, Matt leaned over and whispered in my ear. "Find the conversation dull, love? Me, too. But we'll have some time alone together later. These bigwigs don't have to know everything, right?"

A bird without a head stuck somewhere in my throat.

Was I going crazy or what? It sounded like Matt Gates was coming on to me.

I thought of what Beryl had said about surprising things happening. Yeah, and she'd also said Matt was hot for younger girls. No, I must be getting weak from hunger. Could I be having a mirage, or hearing one, or something?

Maybe my brain needed food. When the dessert arrived, I ate it. It was chocolate mousse and delicious. I decided I *had* imagined Matt's comments, because he was silent again. Mr. Abernathy was talking all about editing the Dream Date evening into a two-minute segment. And Mr. Fieldstone mentioned the flight schedules for the group's trip to London.

"Well," said Mr. Whitehead, "it's after eight. Is our guest of honor ready to move on to Pogo's?"

"I bet she is," said Matt, "and so am I. Let's dance the night away."

Mr. Fieldstone looked concerned. "Now, Matt, you know this whole thing has got to run on schedule. Miss Beaumont must be home by ten."

Matt grinned, then leaned over the table, plucked a white rose from the floral centerpiece, and handed it to me. "This should really be a cornflower to match your blue eyes, but a rose will have to do."

I felt real dizzy when I stood up.

"Something wrong?" asked Mr. Whitehead.

"Wrong? No. Uh, thanks for dinner."

"Our pleasure, young lady."

The pianist in the white tuxedo stood up and bowed as I left. The waiter in the black tuxedo bowed, too. Matt Gates took my arm, and the camera crew followed us out the door.

The people in the main dining room all turned and stared as we passed by. I guess they were far too rich and cultured to scream or get hysterical at the sight of a famous rock star, but they looked impressed. And lots of them also stared at me.

I wished I could've seen myself, too, because I was beginning to get a funny feeling that I wasn't actually there!

Chapter Thirteen

This time, it took *three* limos to get us all over to Pogo's. The camera crew piled into one, the big-deal execs into another, and I was in the last one with Matt and Mr. Fieldstone.

I pulled down the window, letting in some air to clear my head. By now, I was certain I'd imagined my conversation with Matt, because during the drive, he didn't say one word to me.

Mr. Fieldstone did all the talking. "Have you ever been to Pogo's, Jennifer?"

"Never."

"You'll enjoy it. It's not like ordinary clubs. Every two months, Larry Bartlett, the owner, closed up the place for a week to redecorate and create a new theme. This is the opening night of his monsters motif, so it should be especially exciting. As a matter of fact, I know you're in for some surprises."

As our limousine pulled up in front of Pogo's, I saw a crowd assembled around the block, waiting to get in. A short man with long blond hair was pushing them to the side.

"That's Larry Bartlett," explained Mr. Fieldstone. "None of this crowd will make it in tonight. Larry picks and chooses his customers every night and sets a limit. But tonight is even more special. Entrance is very exclusive, by invitation only. But I guess people don't care. Lots of them just like to be seen waiting outside the place."

A long red velvet carpet had been laid down outside the entrance of Pogo's, and Larry Bartlett personally greeted us at the door. Two security guards dressed in wolfman masks greeted us, too.

Mr. Bartlett laughed. "All our performers will be monsters this evening, so don't be surprised at anything, young lady."

But I couldn't help it. The inside of Pogo's looked just like some horror amusement park. The dark, narrow entranceway was covered with cobwebs and phony bats suspended from strings. Inside was a large dance floor with neon lighting underneath, just like in *Saturday Night Fever*, but everything else was really weird.

One part was set up to look like Frankenstein's laboratory, and another, like a torture chamber, with a rack and a skeleton hanging from shackles. In the corner was a large tank of water with a lizard-man swimming inside. Suspended from the ceiling was a trapeze, where a woman dressed up like the Bride of Frankenstein was swinging back and forth.

Lots of people dressed in all kinds of way-out costumes were dancing like crazy—and they were all wearing

93

masks. There was also a giant screen overhead, where clips from old horror movies were being shown. Frankenstein and Dracula, ten times larger than life, were staring down at the masked dancers.

It was unbelievable, like some crazy movie version of a wild Halloween party. There were people in sequins and feathers, and waiters with fright masks carrying trays with wine bottles labeled "blood."

"I've never seen anything like this in my life," I said.

"Good," said Matt. "I want this evening to be filled with firsts for you."

"That's right," added Mr. Whitehead, "enjoy every minute. And have a drink, if you like. It's really cranberry juice."

"Why aren't we being mobbed?" I asked. "I mean, I'm standing here with Matt Gates in person—and no one's running over for an autograph. Don't they recognize you without your sunglasses?"

Matt laughed. "Oh, they all know me. But this is a special invitation party, arranged just for you. The reason we're not being mauled is simple. Everyone here is a famous celebrity—much more famous than I am."

"Really? Who are they?"

"That's my little secret, but believe me, underneath those masks you'll find some of the biggest stars in show business."

It couldn't be, could it? As a man danced by me, I noticed the back of his head looked exactly like Tony Geary. And someone else in a black velvet cape might've been Boy George. And wasn't that Cher underneath the feathered mask? Well, it could've been.

"What're we waiting for?" said Matt. "Let's dance."

By now, my knees were really wobbling. I mean, I couldn't walk out onto that dance floor. Michael Jackson might be staring at me! But I told my knees that this was the biggest moment of my life, so they shouldn't fail me. I was just getting up the nerve to dance when Matt shouted up to the engineer in the sound booth.

"Ricardo, stop the music. The young lady and I want something different, just as I arranged."

Everything stopped dead. For a moment, people stood motionless on the dance floor. Then they slowly moved aside as the sound of a dreamy, romantic melody began filling the room.

Matt took my arm and led me to the center of the floor as the cameraman continued shooting. "Have you ever waltzed, Jennifer?"

"No."

"Wonderful. Then this will be another first."

He took me in his arms, held me tightly, and began waltzing me around the dance floor.

So far, everything had been so wildly wonderful, but so unreal that I still couldn't believe it was happening to me. Now I was sure it wasn't.

I couldn't really be dancing in Matt Gates's arms, could I?

I tried getting a look at myself in the mirrored globes suspended from the ceiling, but I didn't see me, only lots of colored lights.

Was I there at all? Was I really waltzing?

I nestled in Matt Gates's arms. *He* seemed real enough. I could smell the scent of cologne on his cashmere sweater.

I could see the Bride of Frankenstein swinging above my head.

I could see the Mummy drag his bandaged leg across the floor.

I could hear the dreamy music bouncing off the walls.

Dreamy, dreamy waltz music.

That was it: I was dreaming. This was actually Friday night, and I was dreaming about my big date coming up. I could waltz in Matt Gates's arms until my alarm clock woke me up.

At first, I didn't hear it ring. I only heard the sound of violins as my feet glided across the dance floor. But after a while, the sound came, just as I'd supposed: a steady beep, far away at first, then getting closer.

"It's ten o'clock," said Mr. Whitehead, switching off the beeper alarm of his watch. "Time for Miss Beaumont to go home."

"No," I said dreamily, "you mean time to wake up."

"Are you quite all right, Miss Beaumont?" asked Mr. Whitehead. "It really is time to go now."

Suddenly, Matt whirled me across the floor even faster.

"He's wrong, you know," he whispered in my ear. "Old Whitehead doesn't know his fairy tales. Cinderella doesn't have to leave the ball until midnight. And I know just how we'll spend that time. There's a hansom cab waiting out back with a very genial horse and rider, who have instructions to take us through Central Park."

"But I have to wake up—I mean, I have to go home now."

"That's where you're mistaken," he said, whirling me even faster. "This is where your date with me actually begins."

Matt raised his arm, and at that signal, hundreds of balloons suddenly released from the ceiling and began falling in all directions. As the masked dancers ran to the center of the room to catch them, he and I danced faster and faster, until we'd reached the back exit.

There, a hansom cab with horse and driver was parked beside a lamppost, waiting.

"Your coach and horse, milady," said Matt, helping me inside.

Then the carriage raced through the streets, heading toward Central Park.

Chapter Fourteen

Clip-clop, clip-clop went the horses' hooves along the path. The darkened park was deserted except for our hansom cab. The soft spring mist in the air made the lampposts glow with little particles of light. Falling petals from apple and cherry blossom trees filled the air with sweet perfume as the lights from the buildings along Fifth Avenue twinkled through the leaves. A large full moon nestled in the sky next to a million shining stars.

"Our driver thought of everything," said Matt, taking a woolen shawl from the back of the seat. "Here, let me put this around you, Jennifer. There's a chill in the air."

Matt leaned over and draped the shawl around my shoulders. I stared into his sea-green eyes in silence, not wanting to break the mood. If this wasn't a heavenly dream, it was a magic spell, and I couldn't risk breaking it.

"Jennifer, you're so quiet. There's lots of things I want to talk to you about, but you don't seem very talkative."

"You really are here, right?" I whispered.

He laughed. "Yes, love, I'm here and you're here. We're here together. I said I had a surprise for you. Don't you like surprises?"

"Sure I do, but—well, I've never had a date like this before."

"I'm sure you haven't. You don't usually take a dozen other people along on dates, do you?"

"Well, no."

"I wouldn't have called it a date at all—more like a convention. That's why we deserve some time alone."

"What about Mr. Fieldstone and the others? Won't they wonder what happened to us?"

"They know by now. There was a message in each of those balloons. Our masked guests were given instructions to pop them all as soon as they fell."

"What kind of message?"

"It says, 'We're going for a carriage ride. Be back at midnight.' So you see, everything's just fine."

"Midnight? You and me?"

"That's right, you and me, alone together. That business with the balloons was my idea. I guess it was a little dramatic, but I didn't want anyone to know our plans. Those cameramen would be hanging off the back of this horse if they knew!"

I still didn't understand anything. "You really wanted time alone with *me* ?"

"Right. It's no secret that this whole evening was a big publicity event. Well, I got to feeling a little guilty about that, I guess. See, Jennifer, sometimes people in my business can lose sight of reality awfully easily. I try not to let that happen to me, but it's hard when millions of strangers seem to know who you are. Sometimes you start believing you're who they think you are and not who you really are, know what I mean?"

"No, I don't think so."

He smiled. "I think you do. And I think you have a much better idea of what our group represents—I mean, *really*—than most people. You know, making it big in show business when you're young isn't always the best way. Sometimes you can lose track of things like honesty and creative integrity. They tend to get lost in the shuffle of big cars and glitzy parties and publicity campaigns. So I want to thank you for bringing that home to me. You made me see some things straight again. I don't want to be one of those people who looks back after twenty years and asks, 'What's it all mean?' Know what I mean?"

In the moonlight, I could see Matt's green eyes glistening. He was so handsome, so wonderful, so sweet. But I didn't know what he was talking about! "I don't understand; I *love* your music. So does everyone."

He shrugged. "No, Jennifer. Most kids love the hype, the driving beat, and our sexy image. And that's great, terrific; I'm not knocking it. That's what made our album go gold almost overnight. But there's more to our group than that. We have something to say. Sometimes, I wonder if fans ever hear the lyrics, and that can get bloody frustrating. You know, Bryan once said that if I walked out onstage and sang 'Da-doo-da-doo' all night long, we'd get just as much applause. And I was beginning to agree with him—until you came along."

"Me? How did I—"

Matt leaned over and took my hand. "Your *essay*, love. Isn't that what we've been talking about all this time? When I read what you wrote about my music, I knew there was someone out there actually listening."

"My essay? But our English teacher picked the winner. I didn't figure you'd read it."

"Sure, Whitehead sent me a copy. I was curious to know what you thought about my music—and pleasantly surprised."

"You were?"

"Yes, very pleasantly. That's why I arranged this little carriage ride: to thank you personally—and alone. I didn't want all this evening's hype getting mixed up with how I really feel. See, giving you this date wasn't just publicity, it was a pleasure. Know why? Because you've given my music back to me."

"I have?"

"Sure. Your essay touched on all the points I try to make in songs, but I'm never sure if people get them. But after reading what you wrote, I know you understand."

Suddenly, I began shivering under the blanket. It felt like all the blood had been drained from me or something. Matt Gates was saying such wonderful, sincere things that I almost felt like confessing everything.

But how could I? How could I tell him I hadn't written that essay, that it hadn't even been written about his music. It had been written by someone else about someone else. None of it was honest, none of it real. Everything was phony from start to finish.

I tried convincing myself that I didn't tell him because it would've made him feel even more rotten than I did. But that wasn't honest either. I didn't tell him because I didn't have the nerve.

No wonder I'd felt the whole evening had been a dream—as if I'd been a ghost or something. Because *I* wasn't real either. At least, I wasn't the person Matt Gates thought I was.

As our hansom driver continued through the park, the horse at a steady trot, Matt continued talking: how wonderful I was, how my insights had changed all his ideas about teen-agers. And about his new album, too, how he was going to write a new song called "Dream On, Girl," and that it would be all about me.

"A song about *me?*"

"Sure, and I can't wait to see the videotape we made. You looked so wide-eyed, as if everything were a new experience. Like Alice, going through the looking glass, you know? That's what I want to put into words."

Words. I was beginning to hate those five letters!

Suddenly, I started sniffling. I wasn't sure whether I was beginning to cry or getting an allergy attack.

Matt looked concerned. "I guess it's colder than I thought. We'd better get you home now."

I didn't say anything for the rest of the ride; I couldn't. I had to let Matt Gates keep thinking I was the person he thought I was and not who I really was. Because who I really was wasn't anybody, really.

The hansom cab moved slowly through the park, then wound its way up Riverside Drive. But I didn't feel like a princess or a queen any longer, not even when Matt Gates kissed my hand and said good night.

As I stood on the steps of my building and watched the carriage disappear into the night, I suddenly realized what I felt like: Cinderella *after* the ball.

Oh, sure, I was still wearing my pretty blue satin shoes, my rhinestone earrings, and my lovely dress. But I'd turned into a pumpkin, just the same.

Chapter Fifteen

Mom answered the doorbell. "Jenny, I was getting worried. You were supposed to be home ages ago." She stared at me. "You look like a ghost. Are you all right?"

"Sure, I'm fine. Didn't someone call you?"

"Mr. Fieldstone called. He was very apologetic about the plans being disrupted. He said Mr. Gates had left a message in a balloon, saying you'd gone off for a carriage ride. Is that right?"

"Right."

"Well, I guess that was all right. It was, wasn't it?"

For a minute, all the magical, beautiful parts of the evening came rushing back into my mind: the restaurant, the dancers, the feel of Matt's lips against my hand. "Oh, yes, Mom, it was wonderful."

"And what about Matt Gates? What kind of person is he?"

"He was the most wonderful part of all!"

"I'm glad you had a terrific time, dear, but you look tired. I think this Dream Date has been too much for you. Maybe you should get right into bed. Carolyn is staying at Kate's house tonight, so you can sleep late. Tomorrow we can have Sunday brunch together, and you can tell me all the details, okay?"

All the details? I couldn't tell anyone *all* the details. I'd taken my lie too far ever to turn back. "Sure, Mom, I'll see you in the morning."

When I got to my room, I stared at myself in the full-length mirror. I still looked great; a little pale, but great. It seemed weird that I could look so nice on the outside, yet feel so lousy inside. Weren't people's evil deeds supposed to show on their faces? I took a closer look. Nothing.

Say, what was wrong with me, anyhow? I'd had a wonderful evening, right? Matt Gates had had a great time, too. All the girls at school would want to hear about my date. Guys would now be standing on line to date me. And no one knew I'd cheated, so what was the problem?

I undressed and crawled into bed, trying to remember the sound of that dreamy waltz that Matt and I had danced to. I closed my eyes and pretended I was still dancing with him, through chandeliered rooms.

...Dancing with Matt through through fields of flowers, dancing with Matt through heavenly clouds...

But as the waltz continued and Matt spun me around, I suddenly noticed I had no face. I could see my blue pleated dress making swirling motions around my legs, but where my face should've been, there was just a blob. Matt Gates was waltzing with a vacant, empty nothing.

Around eleven, Mom came in to wake me up. "Still in

104

bed? I thought we were having brunch together."

"No, Mom, I'd rather sleep. I'm awfully tired."

"Oh. Recovering from your big night, eh? Okay, but I'm going to the museum, so we'll talk later."

When she'd gone, I locked my bedroom door, hoping to slip back into my dream. It seemed real important that I get back into that fantasy and recover my face.

I grabbed the dream back. This time, Matt and I were in a rowboat, gliding down a lake while moonlight sparkled on the water. He was whispering in my ear, but I wasn't smiling because where my mouth should've been, there was nothing.

Around noon, Carolyn came home and began banging outside. "Why is this door locked?"

"Go away, I'm sleeping."

At one o'clock, Carolyn started banging again. "Jennifer, the phone is ringing off the hook out here. Everyone wants to hear about your date. Aren't you ever coming out of there?"

"*Later*."

Somewhere in that dream world, my face was still floating around and I was determined to find it. So I tried again.

"Jennifer, you beast, come out of there before I break the door down!"

Carolyn.

"What's wrong?" I shouted, jumping out of bed.

"If you don't come out of there this second, I'll set the room on fire!"

"Jenny," Mom shouted, "you'd better unlock that door."

From the tone in Mom's voice, she seemed just as

angry as Carolyn, but why? I checked the clock. It was after three. I must've slept all day. Still, that was no reason to get hysterical. After all, it was Sunday.

As I unlocked the door, I saw Mom and Carolyn standing in the hallway, both looking furious.

"What's the matter?"

Carolyn's eyes were tiny, angry slits, and her face was beet red. "Mother, I'm going to scream! Let me at her!"

"Take it easy," said Mom. "Maybe Jenny has some explanation."

"Explanation? How can you say that? I've been violated—used! *Exploited!* What possible excuse could Jennifer have?"

"Listen, I just woke up, so I don't know what you guys are talking about."

"I'm talking about deceit, theft, and plagiarism! How dare you take my essay—*my essay*—and enter it into that moronically commercial contest!"

So that was it. I was finally hearing the words I'd dreaded. "How'd you find—I mean, what makes you think I did a thing like that?"

"Then it's not true?" asked Mom, hopefully.

"Of course it's true," screamed Carolyn, "so you can't worm your way out of this one, Jennifer. Of all the abysmally wretched things you've done, this is the worst. And just when I was beginning to think you might be seminormal. I should've known the second you entered that contest that there was something fishy. You couldn't win *anything* without cheating your face off!"

"Calm down," said Mom. "Look, Carolyn, I'm just as upset as you are, but let's get some facts first. Jenny hasn't actually admitted stealing your essay as yet. Can't we discuss this like sensible people? Well, Jenny, what have you to say?"

"I'm still awfully sleepy. Can't we talk about this later?"

"What did I tell you?" said Carolyn. "She doesn't even have the guts to admit it. Well, you don't have to, you cretin. I have the evidence."

"What evidence?"

"Barney Weston, that's what. He was one of the many people who called while you were taking your beauty sleep, so I kindly offered to take a message. I don't suppose your peabrain can imagine what he wanted to know."

"What?"

"He said the school paper didn't have enough space to print your entire essay, so he planned to excerpt passages. Then he read me various portions of the masterpiece you supposedly slaved over. Well, I don't have to tell you that it all sounded very familiar. Every single word. You conniving little sneak! You didn't even bother to change one adjective! You turned my thoughtful treatise on the Beatles into a crass commercial venture so that you could spend an evening with that rocker!"

"Don't you are say anything bad about Matt!" I shouted.

"I'll say anything I like, you traitor. You'll never hear the last of this until the day you die!"

"Carolyn, that's enough. Give Jenny a chance to explain."

Explain? Yes, I wanted to explain; to clear my conscience of it, once and for all. "You're right. I stole your paper; I admit it. I want to admit it. Well, I didn't always want to, but then last night I did. But I didn't because I couldn't."

Mom's face grew solemn. "Jennifer, what are you saying?"

"Oh, don't be angry, Mom. I tried writing something on my own, honest I did. But it wasn't any good. And Carolyn is always hammering away at me, telling me what a stupid slob I am, so for once I wanted to prove that I could be a winner."

Mom shook her head. "By *stealing*, Jenny? No one wins by stealing."

"I guess I didn't think of it as stealing; not then, anyhow. And maybe I wouldn't have done it at all if Carolyn hadn't stolen from me first."

"You liar! When have I ever taken anything of yours?"

"How about that stupid paper of yours about subnormal adolescents? Just because I was in an incubator, that doesn't make me subnormal."

"Whoever said it did?" asked Mom.

"Carolyn said so in that sappy term paper of hers. That's right, she said I was subnormal. She even mentioned me by name, so everyone at Columbia could read it. Now all those professors will think I'm an idiot."

Mom's face grew even more solemn. "Carolyn, how could you?"

"I explained it was only a theory: an hypothesis. Besides, I was going to leave out her name in the final draft."

"But even to suggest that your sister might be feeble-minded—you know that's ridiculous. Really, Carolyn, I think—"

"Don't you dare take Jennifer's part in this, Mother! And don't cloud the issue. I refuse to bear any blame for this child's deceitfulness."

"But it's true," I shouted. "You stole, too. You stole my whole life, then mixed it up and shoved it around to fit in with your stupid theories. You *spied* on me, Carolyn, and that's an awful thing, too. Even so, I'm *glad* you know about the contest. I want this whole thing finally to be over."

"I'm sure you do," she said smugly, "now that you've had your big date. But it's not going to be over with that easily. By tomorrow, everyone at Emerson is going to know about this. You won't be able to hold your head up in that school ever again."

"You can't do that! She can't do that, can she, Mom? Don't let her tell everyone."

Carolyn was enjoying her moment of triumph. "It's already done. I informed Barney Weston of the facts, and naturally he doesn't wish to interview you any longer. Instead, he's going to write an exposé of this entire fiasco. Freedom of the press also compels him to tell the principal about it."

"But that's not fair! Mom, there must be some other punishment. I'll scrub the floors for the rest of my life. I'll do everyone's laundry until I'm thirty. I'll get down on my knees and beg!"

"I'm afraid it's too late to change things, Jennifer. Barney Weston called back a little while ago. He'd already informed the principal. Then Mr. Corbett called here. I asked him to wait until I'd spoken to you personally, but now that I have, well, I don't see how you can get out of this. I'm afraid the whole school is going to find out you cheated."

"But you could call Mr. Corbett back, Mom, *please!* Tell him there's been some mistake. Maybe you could say Carolyn helped me a little, that wouldn't be so terrible."

"I can't lie for you, Jennifer. Besides, you miss the point. This goes far beyond you and Carolyn. The fact is, there's some deserving girl at Emerson who wrote an essay that would've—and should've—won that contest. But she didn't because you cheated. You denied someone else a marvelous evening that was rightfully hers."

"But I never thought of it like that, honest. I just wanted to win so badly, I never figured everyone else did, too. I only thought I was stealing from Carolyn."

"I'm sorry, dear. Maybe you didn't realize that's what you were doing, but it's what you did. So we can't cover it up. You're going to have to take the consequences."

Chapter Sixteen

I stayed in my room the rest of the day, just staring at the ceiling, trying to think of some way out of my horrible mess. There wasn't any. If only I could stop time and go back a few weeks, or push it ahead into the future, to a time when all this would've blown over.

But Mom was right. I was going to have to take the consequences. I knew Barney Weston was probably on the phone that very minute telling the whole world the news. Pretty soon, every kid at Emerson would know I'd cheated.

Every friend I'd ever had would turn against me. And all those girls at school, so confident of winning, would know I'd stolen away their big chance to date Matt Gates.

I wasn't surprised when the phone started ringing.

Beryl was the first to call and tell me off. "I was just beginning to like you, Jenny. In fact, I thought we might be friends. Now I'm sorry I told you about all those discount houses, and I guess I should throw out all the makeup I used on your face—or should I say two faces."

But she wasn't the last. Liza called too. "It's not true, is it, Jen? Beryl said Barney told her you'd cheated, and I said it had to be a lie. But Beryl said that Barney said your mother said you'd confessed. Did you?"

"That's right, Liza. I stole Carolyn's essay, so I could win that Dream Date."

"Jenny Beaumont, you're just about the meanest, sneakiest person I ever met."

"No, don't say that. I never thought it'd hurt my friends."

"Oh, really? Jenny, you know I'm a great English student, and I had a real chance of winning that date. To think I called you three times this morning, dying to hear what'd happened last night. Well, now I don't want to know anything about it!"

"But I only thought I was stealing from Carolyn, honest."

"If I were you, I wouldn't use that word."

"You have to believe me, Liza. I never even thought about *you*."

"That's obvious."

"You know what I mean. Listen, everyone else in school is going to hate my guts. You can't be mad at me, too."

"Sure I can."

"Well, at least you have to believe that I didn't mean for things to turn out so awful. You do believe that, don't you?"

"I don't know, Jen. Maybe next week I'll believe it, if I try real hard. But right now, I hate your guts just like everyone else!"

I didn't blame Liza. I didn't like myself any more than she did. If I met myself on the street, I'd probably throw a rock at me or something.

All evening, Mom gave me the silent treatment. And Carolyn left to sleep back at Kate's house, saying she refused to share her room with a "subnormal, subhuman slime-bucket."

I had nightmares all night. Around two in the morning, I got up to take some aspirin, but it didn't help. Even though Carolyn wasn't in the room, I could still hear her threat ringing in my ears: "You'll never hear the last of this until the day you die."

I wanted to die. There was no way I could go back to school and face the music. Dying would be simpler.

Around four A.M., the allergies attacked. Suddenly, my body became a giant scratching post. Everything itched and began to blow up.

When Mom came in to wake me, she didn't seem sympathetic. "Jenny, you're not staying home. Sooner or later, you'll have to face this, so you're only postponing the inevitable. Get up and go to school."

"I can't, Mom, I'm *dying*."

"You're just a little puffy. You always get that way when you're nervous. Take an allergy pill and get dressed. Look, things might not be so bad at school. Some of the kids will give you a hard time, but that's to be expected. You'll have to face them eventually."

"But I'm dizzy and hot and I feel lousy."

Mom felt my forehead. "You *are* hot." She checked my throat and discovered it was flaming red. Then she looked into my eyes. "They're awfully red, too. I'll take your temperature."

It was 102.

Next, Mom rang up Dr. Epstein, the GP in our building, and caught him before he went to his office. He stopped by and officially pronounced me sick: sinusitis, conjunctivitis, various allergies, and a bacterial infection. He wrote out three prescriptions and said I should stay in bed a few days.

Mom called school and explained that I was sick. Before she went to classes, she got my prescriptions filled. Then she called Carolyn to say it might be a good idea if she stayed at Kate's house for a while, until I felt better. Apparently, Dr. Epstein had told her conjunctivitis is very contagious.

"I finish my classes at two," said Mom, "so I'll stop by Emerson to pick up some homework for you. I don't want you falling behind, or you'll never catch up when you go back."

I hoped I was too sick *ever* to go back!

I hid under the covers all day, only getting up to take my medicine. I knew I was avoiding taking my real medicine, namely, facing the world, but I couldn't. Somewhere in my mind, I still kept hoping I wouldn't have to. Dr. Epstein said I should stay in bed a few days. If I could stretch that into a week, well, maybe things might've died down by then. Lots of things can happen in a week, right? I mean, the school might burn down or something.

Sure, I was deluding myself. But the longer I could keep a distance between me and all the kids at Emerson, the better.

When Mom came home with my schoolwork, she also had lots to tell me. "I had a long talk with Mr. Corbett.

114

He's not going to suspend you, thank goodness, but he's sorry he allowed the contest in the first place. He'd hoped it'd be good for school morale, but it's had the opposite effect. Anyway, he thinks the students may have calmed down by the time you're ready to go back. But Mrs. Henley was more upset than he was."

"Henley? You saw her, too?"

"The poor woman said she felt like an accessory to your crime."

"Crime?"

"Plagiarism *is* a crime, Jennifer; a serious one. Mrs. Henley thought it'd be a good idea if you apologized."

"Oh, all right, I'll apologize to her."

"Not to her, to the school—in assembly."

"I'd rather die! What'd Corbett say about that? He didn't agree, did he?"

"Not exactly, but he said some retribution would have to be made. He's considering it. I think he'll decide by the end of the week."

That night, I prayed Corbett would be merciful—and that the week would never end.

The next day, Mom refused to allow me to stay under the covers. "Start working on those homework assignments. That'll keep you busy."

There was a ton of work, but I tackled it. At least it took my mind off my problem.

Through all the gloom, I did have one bright thought. Okay, so maybe all the kids at Emerson knew I'd cheated. But at least Matt Gates would never know. He could go through life using me as his inspiration, thinking of me as his lovely "Dream On" girl.

It was the only nice thing I had left to think about.

That evening, I took a break from schoolwork to watch a little TV. I switched on *Entertainment Tonight* and was only half-watching until I heard the announcer mention Matt Gates.

"And now, the latest in that Dream Date contest," he said. "It seems Matt Gates's big idea to film the winner has backfired. The young lady he escorted around town last Saturday turned out to be an impostor."

What? I switched the sound up louder.

"Yes, folks, the editor of a high-school paper called our studio with this exclusive."

I couldn't believe it. Lousy Barney Weston was on the loose again!

"Luckily, we caught up with Matt just before the group flew to London, and he confirmed the story."

Next, there was a filmed interview with Matt taken at Kennedy Airport. He was wearing his dark glasses and looking very somber.

"Is this true, Matt? Did your date steal the essay that won her the date?"

"That's what I've been told."

"And what's your opinion of that?"

"I'm very disappointed."

"Well, you got some great film footage for your video just the same, right?"

"Wrong. I'm not finishing that video, and I'm not writing that song."

"Why not?"

"I don't want to, that's why. Listen, I can't talk anymore; we've a plane to catch."

After that, there was a short interview with Sidney Whitehead, president of Sandpiper Records.

"What's your opinion of all this?"

"What can I tell you? Matt has integrity. He also has a clause in his contract that gives him final approval on all video material, so what he says goes."

"Well, there you have it, fans. Before Country of the Blind took off for London, Matt told me he'd be rethinking this new album. Whatever he writes next, I'm sure his fans will be behind him. And now, for the latest news about the steaming off-camera romance on *General Hospital*."

I switched off the set, but I could still hear those words: *"I'm very disappointed."*

Now Matt Gates knew the truth, too.

He'd probably hate me for the rest of his life!

I didn't think things could get any worse, but they did.

Carolyn came home.

As soon as she got to the house, she started in on me. "I despise you with a passion, Jennifer. Circumstances make it necessary for us to continue sharing this room, but I'm rearranging the furniture."

Which she did. She took our two dressers and placed them down the center of the room, informing me I was never to set foot on her side—ever. Then she put all the bookcases on top of the dressers, "so I never have to see your pusillanimous, putrid face."

Well, at least I wouldn't have to see hers either.

The rest of the week, I stayed in the house, drowning my sorrows in homework assignments and hoping all my various itises would never go away.

Then on Friday I got the cruelest blow of all.

Mr. Corbett called Mom.

117

He'd made up his mind: I would have to apologize.
On Monday afternoon.
In assembly.
In front of the whole school!

Chapter Seventeen

E ven though I'd prayed it wouldn't, Monday morning
came.

I tried eating breakfast, but it stuck in my throat. All I
could think of was that assembly scheduled for two
o'clock. Two o'clock, when my life would end.

"You have to eat *something*," said Mom.

"I can't. I know they say the condemned always get a
last meal, but I can't."

"Stop being so dramatic," said Carolyn. "This is a perfect
example of cause and effect: every action producing a cor-
responding reaction. Personally, I think this punishment
suitably fits your crime."

Mom banged down her coffee cup. "Shut up, Carolyn!
Enough is enough. Justice is one thing, but revenge is
something else. Stop acting like an *executioner*, and have
a little sympathy for your sister!"

Carolyn looked stunned and sat in silence through the rest of breakfast.

I smiled weakly at Mom. She was doing her best to help me through this ordeal, but no one could help me now.

I was all alone.

As I sat on the bus going to school, I thought of another morning just two weeks earlier. I'd been so eager to get there to find out if I'd won the contest, I'd kept hoping the bus wouldn't crash. Now I hoped it would.

It didn't.

My legs felt like lead as I dragged them up the stairs of Emerson. In the back of my mind, I guess I expected kids to throw rotten eggs and tomatoes or something. But no one threw anything. No one *said* anything. All the kids ignored me. It was really eerie, as if I were invisible or something.

None of the teachers even called on me during my morning classes. I handed in all my English, Math, and history assignments, then spent the time feverishly taking notes, trying to avoid any eye contact.

Lunchtime was even worse. I sat all alone, unable to eat. Luckily, I'd brought a book to bury my face behind. From the corner of my eye, I noticed Liza was now sitting at Beryl's lunch table. Over the noise, I could hear them laughing together. Naturally, I assumed they were laughing at me.

It seemed that the day was lasting an eternity. At first, I'd been hoping two o'clock would never come, but now I couldn't wait for it to arrive. Maybe once I'd officially apologized, people would start treating me like a human again.

There was only one more period to go before assembly. I

handed in my week's biology homework. Mr. Dietrich, the teacher, looked surprised. I guess it was more work than I'd done all year.

Then the assembly bell rang, and we all headed for the auditorium. As dozens of kids pushed their way down the stairs, I finally got some attention. Lots of them glanced over at me and grinned. They knew what was coming up, and they couldn't wait.

But Mr. Corbett had lots of other announcements to make first. There was junk about the bake sale, the science fair, the graffiti in the second-floor bathrooms, and how the renovation of the gym was coming along. I began thinking I was being given that old water torture treatment again. Drip by drip, every drop of courage was draining out of me. When the time came for me to get up, I might not be able to move from my seat. Even worse, I might stand up and faint. Or would fainting be a good thing? No, old Corbett would only schedule another assembly, another day, and I'd have to do it all over again.

"And now," said Corbett finally, "I think most of you know that Jennifer Beaumont is scheduled to address this group. Jennifer, if you'll come onstage, I know we're all anxious to hear what you have to say."

By some miracle, I stood up and walked down the aisle without passing out. I even climbed onto the stage without tripping. But once I was up there, the whole horrible reality of the situation hit me.

I guess you would've thought that'd happened already, but no. As I stood staring out at that sea of faces—friends and former friends, kids who used to like me, kids who never liked me, teachers I hated, and teachers who'd always been nice—I suddenly realized they expected me to *say* something. I mean, more than just "I'm sorry."

And I had nothing else to say.

I really didn't.

In that instant, I realized I should've prepared something. I should've stayed up all night, writing a formal apology, a confession, *something*.

I stared at the crowd in front of me, selecting various faces. Cassie was looking smug. Veronica was giving me dagger-eyes. Mrs. Henley had a look of expectancy. Liza looked sympathetic (I admit it; she did), and Beryl looked a little nervous. But they all looked as if they expected to *hear* something.

I cleared my throat. Then I started to talk, not knowing what I was saying, even after it'd come out. "I— uh—cheated. But I guess you all know that. I know that, too. I mean, I knew I was cheating, but I didn't think I was cheating anyone here at Emerson—but I was. It's not something I can make up for because there's not going to be another contest, so whoever should've won, should've won, not me."

I stared out at the crowd again. Now there was no expression on anyone's face, just hundreds of eyes frozen in my direction.

"But I don't want Mrs. Henley to think it's her fault, because she probably did pick the best essay. I guess calling the contest a Dream Date was true—for me, anyway— because in a way it didn't seem real. Maybe that's because I wasn't supposed to be there. Uh—well, that's it, I guess. I'm sorry."

I heard some coughs, then some giggles. For one horrible second, I thought everyone was going to burst out laughing. But most of the kids just nudged one another or covered their faces with their hands.

I guess Corbett wondered if I was finished or not. So did I. After I'd stood there awhile, not saying anything, he finally came up onstage.

"Yes, well, I guess that's resolved then. You may step down, Jennifer. Now I hope all of us at Emerson can return to more academic concerns. This assembly is dismissed."

As we filed out of the auditorium, Barney Weston was the first to comment. "You sounded like a real jerk up there, Beaumont."

"I didn't think you'd actually do it," said Veronica, brushing past me. "I would've *died* before I made a fool of myself like that."

"You didn't have to tell *me* you cheated," said Cassie, snidely.

I didn't see Liza. She'd probably run out of the building real fast so she wouldn't have to talk to me at all.

Well, I'd done it. But it didn't seem kids were going to start treating me like a human real fast.

Maybe they never would again.

They say confession is good for the soul. Forget it, I didn't notice any difference. Kids still hated me, and I still felt rotten.

Well, there was one difference: now I was starving. I'd had no breakfast or lunch, and my stomach was telling me about it. Mom would be home late, so I had to shop for dinner. I decided to do that on my way home from school. Maybe a major pig-out would make me feel better? Yeah, I'd buy every candy, cake, cookie, chip, and nut I could find. That might help relieve the aching, empty feeling inside—or in my stomach, at least.

When I got to the Red Apple, I piled my cart full of brownies, chocolate chip cookies, corn chips, and peanuts.

"Hi, Jenny," said a voice behind me. "How are you?"

It was Albert.

How was I? As if he didn't know! "That's a lousy thing to say!"

"Huh?"

"How do you think I am? How would *you* be if you'd just made a fool of yourself in front of the entire school?"

Albert pushed his cart to one side and stared at me. "Not so great, I guess. What are you talking about?"

"Don't you know? I mean, the whole world knows. It was even on television."

"What was? *You* were? When?"

"Weren't you in school today?"

"No, not for a week. I've been out sick with the flu."

"Then you"re the only person in New York who doesn't know the news. I stole my sister's essay to win that Dream Date, and Corbett made me apologize in assembly today."

"No kidding! Hey, that's rough. Why'd you do a stupid thing like that?"

I suddenly had an uncontrollable urge to eat. "Because I'm an *idiot*, Albert. But everyone knows that, right? Now leave me alone!"

I banged into his cart, hurried down the aisle, and began dumping my groceries onto the checkout counter.

"Hey, wait up," he shouted, hurrying after me. "I didn't mean *you* were stupid. I meant that whole dumb contest was stupid. But I suppose you shouldn't have cheated."

I couldn't wait for the lady at the checkout to finish packing up, so I grabbed the bag of peanuts and threw some into my mouth.

I was barely out the door when Albert followed after me. "Listen, if you're not in a hurry, I've another idea what you can do with those peanuts."

"Shove 'em up my nose, right?"

He smiled. "No, you did that once, remember? We were in the first grade, and you said your sister told you not to, so you did."

"Oh yeah. Why'd you remember a dopey thing like that?"

"I don't know. Anyway, I thought we might go feed the squirrels. How about a walk in the park?"

"Albert, in case you haven't noticed, I'm lousy company."

"I've noticed. I mean, I don't mind. Well, what do you say?"

"Where in the park?" I asked, not wanting to go anywhere near the Soldier's Monument. Kids from Emerson always hang out there.

"By the river? Unless you think you might throw yourself in."

"Well, maybe I am acting a little wacko. But you would, too, if the whole school hated you."

"So tell me about it. We'll walk down by the water, and you can tell me everything—even about that dumb contest."

"It wasn't a dumb contest."

"Okay," he said, taking my groceries, "but it wasn't the most important thing in the world either, right? The sun still rises and sets, no matter who went out with Matt Gates, right? So c'mon, let's walk."

We headed toward Riverside Drive, then took the path into the park and down to the river, where we sat on a bench to feed the squirrels. As we scattered peanuts onto the ground, squirrels started popping out from behind trees to retrieve them and carry them back into the branches. We didn't say anything for a while, just stared at those squirrels, then out at the water, and I began to feel a little calmer inside.

"Did you really apologize in front of the whole school?"

"Yeah, in assembly."

"What'd you say?"

"I can't remember. Something stupid, I guess."

"Why'd you do it? Steal the essay, I mean. Are you all that crazy about Matt Gates?"

"Oh, that was only part of it. Sure I wanted the date, but more than that, I guess I wanted to be special—just once, anyway."

Albert nodded. "Apologizing took guts."

"Maybe. But everyone still hates me."

"That's rough, but you'll live through it. People can live through lots of rough things, you know."

"Easy for you to say. I bet you've never had to survive a crummy thing like this."

Albert threw a handful of peanuts and watched the squirrels scurry for them. "No, nothing like that. But last year, I thought I wouldn't be able to live through anything. That's when my dad died."

"I'm sorry, I didn't know that."

I thought back, trying to remember Albert's dad. Yeah, he was a real nice guy. In grammar school, on Show and Tell days, he'd always help Albert carry in his tanks and cages. "He was a zoologist, wasn't he?"

"No, a marine biologist. That's where I got my interest in animals, I guess. The last few years before he died, Dad taught at Columbia, but before that he did lots of work at sea. In the summertime, we'd always vacation in the Bahamas where he did research. I really miss those summers together—and our Sundays, too. We did volunteer work at the Humane Society. Now I go alone."

"Sundays? Is that why you didn't go out with me Sunday?"

"Hey, I'm sorry about that. I wanted to take you out, but I couldn't. There was an important animal rights protest in Herald Square."

"Really?"

"Yeah. I'm usually busy Saturdays, too. That's when I stand outside Bloomingdale's."

"Outside Bloomie's? What for?"

"I pass out literature on antivivisection. Sometimes I distribute information protesting the Draize and LD/50 tests, but recently we've been protesting the government's reopening of the Wound Lab."

"What *are* all those things?"

"You've never heard of them? Where have you been all your life? These are important issues. Look, I've got lots of literature about them at home, if you'd like to stop by. Maybe we could have dinner together. My mom has started working two jobs lately, so I usually make myself dinner."

"You do? So do I. Lately, anyway. My mom is studying for her MSW."

"I planned to make French fries tonight. We could make them together. How about it?"

"Sure, I guess so."

"Then let's go."

"Wait. First, tell me what kinds of things you've got living in your house these days. Any lizards, snakes, or beetles?"

"Hey, don't worry. We keep the tarantulas in tanks, and the piranhas are in the toilet bowl. And I've only got a few black widow spiders in the kitchen."

"Albert!"

"Only kidding. Actually, I only have two dogs and a cat. And one of the dogs has no teeth, so you'll be safe."

Albert scattered the remainder of the peanuts onto the ground, then we left the park.

Chapter Eighteen

"Hold it," I said as Albert unlocked the door. "Are you sure there's no creepy-crawlies in there? No roaches with names?"

"There may be roaches, but I don't name them anymore."

I felt a possible sneeze coming on. "I might be allergic to your cat."

"I bet you're not," he said, opening the door.

As he did, a large toothless German shepherd came running toward us, jumped on Albert, and began licking his face. "This is Sascha. She's seventeen, but she still thinks she's a puppy. And that vicious beast heading your way is Clancy."

The cutest, fluffiest, shaggiest little puppy came running

from the kitchen, yapping like mad. As he romped toward me, I noticed he only had one eye.

"The poor thing, what happened to him?"

"A car accident. I found him lying in the street with two broken ribs and a broken leg, too, but he's doing great now. Sascha always wanted a puppy, so she adopted him." Albert glanced around the room. "You haven't met J.B. yet."

Nestled on a pile of sofa pillows, I saw a beautiful blue-eyed Siamese, looking regal as a princess. "She's lovely."

"Yeah, J.B. is the real pedigree in the bunch."

The cat slowly sauntered over and began rubbing herself against my ankles and purring. "What a classy-looking cat. And she's not making me sneeze."

"I told you she wouldn't. You're old friends."

"We are?"

"Sure, don't you remember? I got her four years ago, when she was a kitten. You were here the day Dad brought her home."

"I was?"

"We were ten years old, and you were so excited when you saw her because we hadn't named her yet. You said you'd always wanted something named after you because that'd make you special. So now you're special, Jenny. Meet your namesake."

"J.B.? Jenny Beaumont! Albert, you named her after me?"

"You don't mind or anything, do you?"

"Mind? It's the nicest thing anyone's ever done. And I didn't even remember her."

"That's okay, she likes you anyway. That's because you're a lot alike."

I stared at J.B.'s face. She was the prettiest cat I'd ever seen. "Are we really alike? How, exactly?"

"Well, her eyes, for one thing; they're just as blue as yours. And she loves attention. Sometimes she'll run a-round like a nut just so I'll notice her."

"Thanks a lot!"

"No, I always notice her anyway. I think she's beautiful. But I suppose J.B. doesn't know that. She feels she has to do something special for my attention, when all she really needs to do is be herself."

I think I blushed; at least I felt I had.

"I always noticed you, too, Jenny. Trouble is, you never knew it."

Yeah, I definitely blushed.

"Well, how about those French fries?" he continued. "I'm starving. Should we make something to go with them?"

"Like what? No tofu, thanks. And I don't like sunflower seeds either. They stick between my teeth."

"How about fish sticks? That's easy."

"Fish? I thought you were a vegetarian."

"Lots of vegetarians eat fish and eggs. I only object to meat."

We went into the kitchen and the animals followed. All three of them settled underneath the table and watched as we got dinner started. I began peeling as Albert poured some oil into the fryer.

"My mom says all the vitamins are in the skins," said Albert.

"So does mine, but I still won't eat them. How is your mom these days?"

"Okay. I guess she's adjusting. She still misses my dad,

of course, but like she says, life goes on. She really felt rotten when I had to drop out of private school, but she couldn't afford the tuition. But if I keep my grades up, I'll probably get a scholarship to a good college, so that's okay."

"Well, at least you've made friends at Emerson."

"Some."

I sliced up the potatoes and dropped them into the fryer basket while Albert put the fish sticks on a cookie sheet and stuck them in the oven.

"I mean, you and Beryl are good friends now, right?"

Albert slammed the oven door. "You know, sometimes I think you're trying to push Beryl on me, but I can't figure out why."

"You have to admit she's pretty."

"Sure she's pretty. But I didn't go out and buy new clothes and have my hair cut to attract Beryl."

"What?"

"That day at the movies. I suppose you didn't know I'd fixed myself up so you'd notice me. Oh, I've heard what Liza calls me—Buggy Bertie. She usually says it so loud, I can hear it down the hall. I guess I was trying to change my image to impress you."

"You did that for *me*, Albert? You didn't have to."

"You mean I shouldn't have bothered, right? Yeah, I suppose I'll never live down that date we had in grammar school when I took you to the museum."

"I don't remember that," I lied. "Did we have a good time?"

"Terrible. I must've bored you to death."

"No, you didn't. I think dinosaur bones are fascinating."

"Hey, I thought you didn't remember."

"Well, it's coming back to me. On our way home, you bought us double-scoop ice cream cones, but you fed most of yours to a stray cat."

Albert looked embarrassed. "A real nerd, right?"

"No, you were nice, but I did think you were a little bit like Dr. Dolittle."

"Terrific. And I always figured I was just like Albert Schweitzer. That's who my folks named me after— reverence for life and all that stuff."

"Well, that's stuff's wonderful, I admire it. I mean, you'd never pick a person's brain or treat someone like a guinea pig, would you? I'll bet you only treat guinea pigs like guinea pigs."

Albert glanced at me as he took some dishes from the cupboard. "Am I supposed to understand that remark?"

"Guess not. I suppose I mean you're fine just the way you are."

"Really?"

"Sure. So I wouldn't worry about what Liza says. She's not the smartest person in the world, you know. Most of the time, all she wants to do is talk about clothes and cosmetics."

Albert put down the plates, suddenly remembering something. "After dinner, remind me to give you some flyers. Once you read them, you'll never use makeup again. Know how they test those cosmetics you wear? By force-feeding them to animals and blinding rabbits."

"Please, not on an empty stomach."

"But consumers have to know this stuff. We can make a difference, Jenny. If enough people protest, the cosmetic industry will have to come up with alternatives."

"Can't we wait until we eat our French fries?"

"I guess I get carried away, but I can't help it. When I see people wasting their time on unimportant stuff, when there are so many things we can all do to make this world better, I get impatient."

"And I suppose you think cheating in a Dream Date contest is really unimportant stuff, right?"

"Well, it won't change the world, will it? Pretty soon, kids at Emerson will be excited about some other stupid thing instead, and they'll forget all about what you did."

"You really think so?"

"Sure. By next week, no one'll remember you."

"Thanks!"

We could smell the fish sticks were ready, so we dumped them onto a platter. And the French fries were brown and sizzling. Albert fed little pieces of potato to Sascha and Clancy, while I watched J.B. take dainty nibbles of fish from my hand. As I ate, I kept staring at her, thinking that Albert had named her after me—and that he thought she was beautiful.

After dinner, we washed up, then Albert dumped a ton of flyers and pamphlets onto the table: piles of literature on animal rights and antivivisection. He really became intense when he started talking about it. I knew he was informing me of extremely yucky things, but I couldn't help noticing how marvelously strong and determined he looked.

"I guess you're a true crusader."

"You can be a crusader, too," he insisted. "Animal rights needs all the help it can get."

"Me? What can I do?"

"Write to cosmetic companies, picket, protest, hand out flyers." He looked up from the pile of papers and stared into my eyes. "Why do you need makeup anyway? You're beautiful without it." Then he leaned over and kissed me: the nicest kiss I'd ever had. He held me in his arms as J.B. brushed against my legs and purred. I felt like purring, too.

Then Sascha began howling and jumping up to separate us.

"She has to go out," he said. "Okay, old girl, get your leash."

Sascha went running from the kitchen, returning with two leashes and Clancy in tow.

"Have you time for another walk in the park?" asked Albert.

"Sure."

We walked down by the river again. The lampposts were on now, and a light spring mist hung in the air. The squirrels had retreated into the trees, but we could hear the cries of sea gulls flying over the water as they chased a tugboat pulling a garbage barge. The lights from the tug reflecting on the water made it seem like the most romantic garbage barge I'd ever seen.

Sascha pulled at her leash, but Albert restrained her. "She loves to run around loose, but they've dumped rat poison down here again."

I looked into Albert's eyes. "Really? That's nice."

"What?"

"I mean, that's terrible."

He laughed, and then we kissed again.

"I've never liked anyone as much as you, Jenny. Not since first grade when you tricked me into giving you all my Matchbox cars."

"I didn't."

"You did. You said your sister stole yours, so I felt sorry for you."

"You did? That was awfully nice of you, Albert."

"I'm a nice guy. The only reason I looked forward to coming to Emerson is because I knew you went there. And Beryl Fleming, of course. No, I'm just kidding. It was you I was interested in—always. That's why I kept pestering you to help with your homework."

We kissed again, then we sat down on a bench to stare out at the water while Sascha and Clancy played with a fallen branch. There was something about my being with Albert that I hadn't noticed before. He made me feel quiet and good inside, as if I'd just stepped out of a warm bath and into clean clothes.

We sat there like that for a few minutes, holding hands. Albert put his arms around me, and I stared into his eyes. They weren't gray-green after all, but pure green—like the ocean, like emeralds, like the forest—and I could see myself reflected in them.

Me, Jenny Beaumont, just as I was.

Chapter Nineteen

Carolyn was her usual charming self when I got home.

"Where've you been? I'm *starving*. You were supposed to make dinner."

"Dinner? No thanks, I've already eaten. Fish 'n' chips—delicious."

"I'm talking about *my* dinner."

I dumped all the brownies, cookies, and corn chips onto the table. "Here, pig out."

"What kind of meal is this, you birdbrain?"

"Thanks for the compliment," I said. "You know, a bird's brain is comparatively large for its size. If you'd studied your biology, as I have, you'd know that."

"What's gotten into you? Did you go to school today? If you didn't, I'll find out about it."

"Oh, I went. Apologizing wasn't that big a deal after all. So now we're straight, right? My punishment fit my crime, and all that junk."

Carolyn glared at me. For once in my life, I felt I might

have the upper hand. She seemed speechless, and I couldn't let the precious moment pass me by.

"Well, maybe not quite straight," I added. "You still owe me for all those Matchbox cars you stole in first grade."

"Matchbox cars? What's the matter with you?"

"Nothing. But I think I've discovered *your* problem in my biology book. Did you know that the surface of a baby's brain takes four years to develop? And the insulating membrane that surrounds the nerve cells aren't complete until adulthood. I think that's what's wrong with you, Carolyn. Your myelin membrane isn't fully developed yet."

Carolyn's face grew so red, I thought she'd explode. "Same to you, jerk!" she shouted, then slammed the kitchen door behind her.

Later that night, Liza called me.

"Hi, Jen. Just wanted to let you know that it's next week."

"What? Oh! You mean you don't hate my guts any-more?"

"Maybe not. One thing's for sure: I couldn't have stood up like that in front of the whole school—not even for *two* dates with Matt Gates. Want to have Cokes at Charlie's tomorrow?"

"Sure, Liza, *thanks*."

"What're friends for?"

Albert called around eleven. "I didn't wake you, did I?"

"No, what's up?"

"Nothing. I just wanted to tell you I had a great time tonight."

"Me, too."

"Want to go out with me on Saturday?"

"Sure, what'll we do—stand outside Bloomie's together? We can say rotten things to all the women wearing fur coats."

He laughed. "No, I thought we might go to a movie."

"That sounds like fun, too."

"Swell. Good night, Jenny."

" 'Night, Albert."

I washed up, got into bed, and lay there thinking of my date with Albert that was coming up.

I knew it would be a dream date—a *real* one, this time.